Broken

Broken

Kayt C. Peck

SAPPHIRE BOOKS

SALINAS, CALIFORNIA

Editor - Kaycee Hawn
Book Design - LJ Reynolds
Cover Design - Fineline Cover Design

Sapphire Books Publishing, LLC
P.O. Box 8142
Salinas, CA 93912
www.sapphirebooks.com

Printed in the United States of America
First Edition – September 2020

This and other Sapphire Books titles can be found at
www.sapphirebooks.com

Dedication

To my sisters and brothers, my fellow Veterans and
First Responders. This story is my gift to you. In some
small way, I pray it gives a modicum of healing to at least
some of you and, perhaps, some greater understanding
for those who love and support you.

Acknowledgments

My special thanks to Chris and Schileen at Sapphire Books and to their crew of editors and designers. Like all art forms, whether or not it will actually be seen and appreciated is all in the presentation. I value also my growing circle of sister writers who think in terms of love and support, helping each other to create the best art possible. They share my belief that the creation of magic is not and never should be about competition.

Chapter One

Awakening

The sheets wadded around her, leaving her feeling as trapped in the bed as her mind was in the dream that haunted her. Again and again, the same dream, the same dream, the same dream—the nightmare she'd lived once and relived far too many nights. Mel prayed for an ending, for the memory she could not recall. Would the dreams end? Would they truly end if she could unlock the door to that piece of her mind where something mysterious lay buried?

Her left foot itched, and Mel groaned in frustration. There was no foot to scratch, making the itch a tormenting hint of what purgatory must be. She used a technique she'd learned while in recovery at Bethesda, one taught not by a physical therapist or doctor, but by a fellow vet, an old man, his own leg lost decades before in Southeast Asia. They'd both been outside, wheelchair bound, breathing fresh air and feeling sunshine, which Mel gobbled at like a starving woman handed a loaf of bread. Too long she'd been trapped in a field tent, then hospital ship, then the hospital itself. The spring morning felt wonderful, but her foot itched, the one she no longer had. From a few feet away, the old man looked up and watched as she lifted her leg, the one that ended like an incomplete sentence. She scratched tenderly, desperate to end the itch but mindful of the still healing flesh.

"Find the line," he said with a shaky voice.

She looked at him for the first time, seeing a yellowish face, one that spoke of the alcohol that had helped him survive the years.

"What line?" she asked.

"Nerves go in a line. Find the one that led to your foot. Scratch up it 'til you find the right spot."

Feeling a tad foolish but ready to try anything, Mel did as he instructed. She started near the stump, surprised that she instinctively knew she'd found the right "line." Up she went, scratching along the way—up the calf, then thigh, along the hip and to her stomach until she found a spot that, like magic, felt exactly like she was scratching the phantom foot. She sighed in relief.

"Thanks," she said. She grasped the metal hand rim attached to the chair's wheels and deftly maneuvered closer, facing the man. "That's a good trick. I appreciate you sharing."

"We're all in this together," the man answered. He pointed to her left leg. "That will get better." His eyes were an intensely faded gold as he looked her full in the face. "Have the dreams?"

Mel's breath caught in her throat. "Yes," she answered, ashamed of the break in her voice.

"Those may not," he added.

He'd been right.

Mel found the spot on her stomach, one she could now find without searching and scratched the phantom foot, eliciting a sigh of relief. Using her good leg, she kicked at the covers, breaking free of their bondage. She swung around to sit on the side of the bed. Ignoring the prosthesis hanging from a bedpost, she hopped the few feet from the bed to the door of the master bathroom. She paused, leaning on the doorframe for a moment before hopping again to the toilet to pee then to the sink where she gripped the sides of the porcelain, taking unexpected comfort in the cold, smooth surface. She looked in the mirror at the dark circles under her eyes, a fresh streak of gray beside her right temple, adding a new dimension to the auburn of her hair. Her face still reflected the beauty that had been a blessing and a curse all her life, but there was a gauntness. A haunting, oddly beautiful in its own way, replaced the passion in the blue of her eyes, but her reflection held a strangeness for her. She wondered who this woman was. Gone was Navy Captain Melinda Morris. She saw a shadow of that confident, courageous woman, one whom she'd been proud to know, proud to be.

"Broken," she whispered. "You're broken," she said to that stranger in the mirror. Then she saw a flash of anger in the reflected blue of the eyes. She grasped a glass on the shelf below the mirror and launched it toward the linen closet door, smiling viciously at the rewarding sound of breaking glass.

"I'll whip this, you hear me!" she yelled into the mirror, jabbing at the image with a forefinger. Then her voice took on a softer note as she looked sympathetically at the reflected face. "We'll whip this."

Mel shook her head then turned the cold water on full blast, leaning toward the sink to splash her face, hands, and arms. She brushed her teeth, using her cupped hand for water to rinse the froth away, improvising with the absence of the now broken glass. She swiveled on her only foot toward the door, pausing as she looked at the broken glass scattered between her and her only egress.

"Shit," she mumbled. "That was stupid."

She grasped the edge of the sink for support and lowered herself to the floor, pulling a trash container toward her with one hand and a small towel from the rack beside the sink with the other. She carefully picked up the large shards of glass, placing them in the container, systematically following behind with the damp towel to retrieve the smaller pieces from the floor. By the time she'd ooched all the way across to the door, the glass was retrieved, and she felt it was safe to stand. She threw the towel on top of the glass in the container and set it to the side, knowing she could now add it to the large trash can on the service porch that she would later take to the rural dump station ten miles away, one that served farms and ranches within a twenty mile radius. Mel used the doorknob to pull herself to a standing position, once again ignoring the prosthesis hanging from the bed post. She hopped to the closet and, from a shelf, pulled another prosthesis from where it rested beside a well-worn running shoe. The left shoe rested beside it, not as worn. She threw the shoe and spring-like pseudo-foot onto the bed then pivoted to the dresser where she pulled fresh, clean running shorts, t-shirt, sports bra, underwear, and a single sock from a drawer.

Shorty pajamas were abandoned, and Mel dressed quickly, craving the run that she knew would clear her mind and ease the pain of her heart. For much of her life, running had been her go-to when life was too much, whether it be pain or joy. Only time spent on the back of a horse had ever surpassed the simple comfort and ecstasy she found in running. Well, not the only thing. Mel shook her head, pushing that thought aside. She wasn't ready to think of a woman, any woman. Even as fantasy, the possibility of the level of pleasure of soft flesh, smooth skin, and the intensity of simple arousal seemed too far away, too unattainable—too vulnerable. Some days, most days actually, she still managed to function by keeping the flood of emotions behind a dam of self-control. To lower the floodgates, even for the prospect of love, risked a deluge of emotional pain that could drown her, and she knew it.

"Whatever happens, sweet Melinda, the ranch is here. Come home if you need us." Mel heard her father's voice through the echoes of memory. It had been at the airport as he'd seen her off, a frightened young woman, her college sheepskin still fresh, leaving for a twenty-five-year adventure as she entered Officer Candidate School for the US Navy.

He was dead now; a heart attack abruptly ended his presence as the cornerstone of the family. Her mother lived in a nursing home; the Alzheimer's had finally become more than her brother and sister-in-law could manage on their own. Her parents were gone, but her father had been right. The ranch was still there, and she'd come home. She had come home broken. The house and the room that had been her parents' was now hers. The New Mexico prairie had been her first love, but the sea had been her life. No longer. She must fan the coals of her love of the land. It had sustained her once. She prayed it would again.

Mel stood abruptly, unable to overcome decades of Navy habit as she fought to control the chaos of covers caused by her restless night. Finally, the bed was made, ship-shape. She bounced a time or two as she finished the task. She smiled, pleased at the surprising exhilaration she felt at the motion made possible by the prosthesis specifically designed for her as a runner. She bounced out of the bedroom and past the kitchen, pausing only for a quick glass of orange juice. Breakfast would come later. She knew she needed to eat or face the nagging of a well-intended sister-in-law, troubled at the weight Mel lost during her long recovery. She had always been fit and lean, a fact that had been somewhat detrimental during her recovery. A few extra pounds would have been a nice reserve.

The screen door slammed behind her as she stepped outside. The horses were out to pasture and the chicken house was empty, so there were no chores to delay her sprint into the cool of the morning. Mel headed out of the driveway and down the county road, knowing there would be no traffic to slow her. Only three ranches had headquarters along this road, and the nearest was five miles away. As she felt the rush of air around her and the motion of her own body, for a time, all the pain, the nightmares, the grief were forgotten. She was lost in the animalistic joy of motion, of the thump of her heart and the rhythm of her running steps, actually enhanced by the artificial foot that gave her extra power.

But prostheses are made for city sidewalks or cinder tracks, not rutted caliche roads. The tip of the spring foot caught a clod in the road, and Mel's joyous run turned into a tumultuous fall. As she lay in the dirt, she realized more than her body had crashed. Perhaps it was having achieved a momentary high that made the unexpected fall so tragic. Despite a life-habit of determination and courage, despair covered Mel like a suffocating blanket. Not for the first time, she remembered the 9mm in her nightstand drawer. How easy it would be to end the pain.

"You're a Morris." Mel heard her father's stern voice through the ears of memory. "And we don't give up."

She remembered the first time she heard that litany. Her father had dried her childish tears, checked her for broken bones, then set her on her feet and simply pointed at the paint pony that had so recently dumped her. Five-year-old Mel had sniffled, but she got back on the horse.

Mel stood, looked at the blood on her arm from a long scrap from elbow to wrist.

"I hear you, Daddy," she mumbled.

The run home was slower, hampered by a limp, but she ran. After all, she was a Morris, and they don't give up.

Chapter Two

Daymares

The coffee was even stronger than the sludge commonly found in a ship's galley, and Mel loved it. Periodically, her duties at Navy Central Command brought her to Bagdad, a city she'd grown to love. She mourned deeply the damage to both the city and its people by the long presence of war. She always managed to sneak in a visit to this coffee house, near a market from which she could hear the bustle and drone of barter and business, much as it had been practiced in this city for millennia. The sounds gave her hope that Bagdad would survive, just as it had so many wars before.

Her official business had been brief, simply checking on the status of a supply depot which serviced many of the U.S. and allied military commands stationed in Iraq. She and her aide, Lieutenant Harold Canton, had made short work of the inspection and material review. It didn't take long to know that the Marine major and his crew knew what they were doing. She and Canton had stopped as they crossed through the edge of the city, heading for the airfield where a plane waited to take them back to Bahrain. Canton left her alone at the table, his cup growing cold, as he went in search of the head, something that could be a challenge with the language barriers. He may be gone for a while.

Open before her on the table was Mel's ever-present notebook, and she scribbled reminders about what she wished to include in her report to Central Command. She took no notes about her other meeting, the secret meeting. Zadab, her lover of fifteen years, had a beloved cousin, Sherine, who now headed an organization that sought to protect Iraqi women, especially those targeted for honor killings. Any time Mel came to Baghdad, they would meet, and Mel would do what she could, even if it was only to pass along a knick-knack or family news from Zadab. They would meet in the same place, the backroom of a small shop. Sherine could not afford to be seen in the company of a U.S. Navy captain, not with the animosity felt by so many Iraqis because of the American "occupation." Mel's commander knew and approved of the contact, and she was careful to officially, if secretly, report on her meetings, a path which the admiral hoped would help, in time, to improve relations with the women of Iraq.

Mel paused, feeling the heft of the pen in her hand. Her thoughts drifted back to that birthday when she and Zadab had actually both been home, sharing daily life in their Virginia suburb. Her birthday consisted of dinner at her favorite restaurant, a movie, and the company of the woman who was her companion and best friend. Zadab presented the pen to Mel over dinner, and that moment remained in Mel's mind as a precious memory. As lovers, their relationship had always been lukewarm, but that hadn't mattered much. Both were more married to their work than each other. In an odd way, it made their relationship deeper, if somewhat difficult to define. Mel always carried the pen, an expensive writing instrument. The feel of it in her hand reminded her that she had a home, a place where she could truly rest and know she was safe.

Stretching tired muscles, Mel laid the pen on the table as she reached far over her head, striving to ease the tension in her neck. She hadn't noticed that the table was not level, and the pen rolled, falling from the edge, evading Mel's efforts to capture it. She sighed as she watched it roll to the base of a concrete pillar that supported the roof which shaded the open-air café. She rose from her chair, took a stride, stretching to retrieve the pen, her left foot extended beyond the edge of the pillar. She grasped the precious pen in her hand, relieved to see it was undamaged.

Then the world ended.

Reality rushed past Mel at the speed of light, leaving her momentarily deaf and blind, and barely aware of excruciating pain that overwhelmed her senses. In the time it took to take half a breath, the café transformed from a pleasant oasis in a war-torn land, to the epicenter of destruction itself. Despite the protection of the concrete pillar, the concussion of the explosion alone sucked the very air from Mel's lungs, and left her ears hopelessly plugged from the abrupt change in air pressure from normal air to intensely dense to normal air again as the flash of the explosion passed. Clutched in her right hand was the pen, the wayward pen that had saved her life. She lay in the rubble, confused and disoriented, her eyes focused on a wall across the way, and she watched as the earthen bricks, formerly covered by stucco, teetered and finally fell in a domino effect that took her back to a teenaged memory. Her brother, Hoyt, had failed to balance a stack of fresh hay, and it had toppled in a slow-motion taunting of her brother's efforts. Insanely, she fought laughter, recalling how she and her father had teased a frustrated Hoyt.

The pain found its way past the initial shock, and she raised her left leg to determine how badly she was injured. Her foot and ankle were gone with the top three inches of her combat boot still hanging tenaciously to the stump. Blood flowed from the opening, and Mel's intelligence and training stepped in to overpower the euphoria of shock. She undid her belt buckle and pulled the belt free, hampered by the pen in her hand. Despite the threat, she took a moment to carefully stow the pen, her lifeline, into a pocket of her BDU blouse. She wrapped the belt just above the bleeding stump and twisted, grasping a shard of wood from the rubble, to place at the top of the twist. When tight enough to slow the flow of blood, she tucked the sliver of wood underneath the band around her leg before dipping her finger in her own blood and painting a "T" on her forehead. Her training held, even in trauma. That "T" would let the corpsmen know a tourniquet was hiding under the blanket they may use to save her precious body warmth. She lay back, wondering if unconsciousness would come soon, masking the intensity of her pain.

Canton! Where's Canton? She thought, praying that the young lieutenant had been safe from the explosion. That was when her hearing returned. A sound, incongruous in the devastation of war, left her feeling even more disoriented.

A toddler's cries wailed, louder than the moans she heard from others injured. She rotated her head, striving to triangulate the sound with her still limited hearing. It was then she remembered the Iraqi couple, a small boy in the mother's lap, all sitting at a table near her own. She turned her head and fought the urge to be sick at what she saw. Half the father was simply gone; the dirt and charred black from the explosion marred the white of the clothing, covering what remained of the body. Amazingly, there was no blood on the clothing, only the tell-tale red where his upper half had been severed from the bottom. There was no sign of the rest of the man. The woman's body was ravaged as well, although she had been partially protected by the same concrete pillar which saved Mel. One solid, open wound replaced what had once been her back and the back of her head. She lay tightly balled, some obstruction obviously beneath her. The sounds of a wailing child came from beneath her mangled body.

Mel pulled herself inch by inch toward the woman and the child still protected beneath the mother, pausing now and again to push aside a piece of rubble that blocked her path. When she reached them, Mel struggled to push the body away and retrieve the crying child. Shocked, she felt movement, as the mangled mother sought to help her, raising slightly on one arm. Mel pulled the child—miraculously with no apparent wounds—toward her as she looked into the fading eyes of a dying woman.

Mel opened her mouth to speak.

≈੪ ≈੪ ੪≈ ੪≈

Soaked in sweat, Mel awoke. She lay atop her bed, still in much the same position she had assumed when first reclining for an afternoon nap. Tears joined the salt of the sweat on her face.

The same damn place, Mel thought. *The dream always ends in the same damn place. Why can't I remember?*

Mel sat on the edge of the bed and reached for the prosthesis where it hung on the bedpost. She placed it in her lap then froze and closed her eyes. A stew of emotions bubbled in her heart and mind, and she sat perfectly still, letting the hodge-podge of feelings swish around in her mind, like holding a mouthful of casserole on the tongue, striving to identify the subtle spice, giving it a unique flavor. Pain, fear, and anger were all there, dominant flavors, but there was something else, something that felt like it might be the source of the wall that kept her dreams and her memories from moving forward, completing the horrific story of the worst day of her life. When the nature of that elusive emotion floated to the top, puzzlement joined it.

Guilt, Mel thought. *Why guilt?*

She threw the prosthesis on the bed and hopped, one-legged, into the bathroom, turning the cold water on full blast at the sink. She threw handfuls of piercingly cold well water on her face, even the back of her neck. It helped. The breathtaking cold reminded her she was alive.

The woman staring back at her in the mirror seemed strange. She was thin with dark circles under her eyes. Mel could barely recognize the confident and determined Naval officer whom she knew so well and admired.

"What did you do?" she mumbled to the image. "Why guilt?"

She looked away from the mirror toward her

hands, clutching desperately to the porcelain of the sink. The grip on such solidity was the only thing that kept them from shaking uncontrollably.

What did I do?

☙☙☙☙

Looking at the surface of the coffee in her cup, Mel frowned at the ripples she saw there. Her hand was shaking, and she hated that. The fresh, spring air comforted her as she sat on the open front porch of the family ranch home, but the dream—the pervasive dream—still haunted her. The physical disability that all could see barely troubled her anymore. It was the incomplete memory—that fucking dream—that drove her to the solitude of the ranch and left her feeling as unfit company for any other human being.

The cell phone vibrated on the patio table beside the chair where she rested.

I actually have good cell signal today, Mel thought as she picked up the phone. The music she'd chosen for the ring tone gave her comfort, even before she answered.

"Hey," Mel said.

"We don't talk for a week and you answer the phone 'hey'?" Zadab answered.

"Sorry Hon…" Mel started, then caught herself, "Zadab. Still feeling my way around our new situation."

There was a pause before Zadab responded. "I will always love you," she said.

"But not in love with me."

"No," Zadab said. "Were we ever 'in love'?"

Mel tried to choke back a bitter laugh, with little success. "No, we weren't, but I will always love you too."

"Are you taking care of yourself?" Zadab asked.

"Of course," Mel responded. She took a deep breath. "How's Lelia?"

"We are good, Mel, but I suspect you are lying about taking care of yourself."

"Doing the best I can," Mel responded. "How does Lelia feel about your calls to me?" she asked in an effort to change the subject.

"She's a little uncomfortable, but she understands." Zadab gave a sigh. "One day you two will be friends."

"I'm not there yet, Zadab."

"I know. Neither is she. Give it time."

The pause was comfortable. The two women had learned long ago to be comfortable with each other's silence. Their complicated relationship had survived largely because each understood the complexity of the other's life, the weight of their responsibilities, and never resented the times when they each escaped into the world inside themselves. During that pause, Mel processed for the thousandth time how the end of her marriage contributed to her current state.

Her life with Zadab was as broken and absent as her left foot. Her partner of fifteen years was gone. Zadab had been with her, stayed loyal and supportive every step of the way, through the surgeries, the skin grafts, the healing, the physical therapy, the customized creation of prostheses that would give Mel's life a semblance of normalcy. Only when it came time to leave the hospital, to go home, only then did Mel learn that home was now an empty place. Zadab had found another. In a sense, not much had changed. Mel and Zadab had always been bound by love but not in love—by mutual respect for the work that consumed both their lives, Mel in the Navy and Zadab as an interpreter with the Department of State. They maintained a deep friendship based on a profound caring begun so long ago.

Mel had interceded in a coffee shop as Zadab stood courageous and unflinching before three men offended by the hijab she wore. Dressed in her Navy khakis, golden oak leaves on her collar and ribbons on her chest, Mel had always assumed it was respect for the uniform more than anything else that changed the bullies' tone as she stepped in to defend a beautiful Iraqi/American woman. Between Mel's deployments and Zadab's travels as an interpreter, there were years they had been lucky to be together more than three or four months of the twelve, but they had been an anchor for each other. If the passion was limited, the respect was not. Try as she might, Mel could not deny Zadab the joy of finally finding heart-churning happiness in the arms of another. She could and did feel envy, but not anger, not jealousy, no sense of betrayal. But Zadab and the townhouse that had been home, that was gone.

"Are you still there?" Zadab asked. The pause had gone on long enough that the cell line sounded dead.

"Yeah, just thinking," Mel said.

"You doing anything else or just spending time with too much thinking?" Zadab asked.

"Went for a run this morning," Mel answered. She lifted her arm and looked at the long, angry scratch from wrist to elbow, incurred during her fall. That she did not mention to her former wife, her best friend.

"Good," Zadab said.

Mel's attention to the call was distracted as she watched a white pickup truck in the distance, turning off the highway and down the dusty county road that ran beside her house.

"I need to go," Mel said. "Someone's coming."

"Hoyt?" Zadab asked, mentioning Mel's brother.

"No."

Confusion could be heard in Zadab's voice, even through the cell signal. "To the ranch? Who could it be? Oh Allah, I hope it's not a Jehovah's Witness."

"Not likely. Looks like a repair truck. It has racks and a ladder across the top. Besides, you know I'm in the Jehovah's Witness protection program."

"I know. You pull out the *Quran* faster than I do when they come to the door."

"Works every time." The truck was slowing, obviously heading for Mel's house instead of the neighbor ranch further down the road. "He's nearly here. I better see what's up."

"Take care, Mel, and call me now and again."

"Uh, I prefer you call me. Don't want Leila to get the wrong idea."

"As long as you promise to call or have Hoyt call if you need me," Zadab said.

"Promise," Mel said. "Bye for now."

As Mel hit "end" on the phone, the truck pulled into the driveway. Mel could see the peeling "Dallan Satellite Service" on the passenger door. The truck stopped in the driveway near the house. A bearded man stepped from the truck and walked toward Mel.

"Well, if it ain't Melinda Morris in the flesh," he said, a broad smile half hidden in the salt and pepper beard.

Mel set her coffee cup on the table and stood, a smile lighting up her own face.

"Dang, Tom Henderson! How the heck are you? Didn't recognize you behind that beard."

The man laughed and patted a rather ample stomach hanging over the belt of his work jeans. "Beard and another fifty pounds since high school."

Mel met him half-way, and they exchanged a hearty hug at the base of the porch steps. When Mel stepped back, he glanced quickly, an apparent reflex, at the exposed metal of her artificial foot. His effort to look away was obviously forced.

Mel chuckled. "Want to see it?" she asked. "It's a miracle of modern technology."

"Well dang, can't blame a man for being curious."

"Not one bit," Mel answered. "Want a cup of coffee?"

"Naw, I got plenty left in the thermos in my truck. Wife makes it just the way I like it."

Mel motioned for him to take a seat beside the patio table, then moved her chair so he could clearly see her prosthesis as she raised the leg of her jeans, showing the entire metal portion.

"This is my plain old walking foot," she said. "I've got another one that's basically a titanium spring. Makes running feel like I could fly."

"If you'd had it in high school, Dallan High School's women's track team would have taken state all four years instead of just two."

"Wouldn't want to be greedy," Mel responded, smiling at the shared memory.

Tom cleared his throat. "No kidding, Melinda. I was plumb sorry when I heard what happened."

"I was military all my adult life, Tom. I knew the risk."

"Still don't make it easy," he said.

Mel leaned back and took a drink of her cold coffee, making a face when she realized the temperature.

"So, is this a social call while you're in the neighborhood?" Mel asked.

"Nope. Here to install satellite TV and internet," he said.

"I didn't order it, Tom."

"I know," he answered. "Hoyt did. Said he didn't want you going stir crazy and coming after him with a baseball bat."

"My brother knows me too well."

Tom's face turned serious. "No place like home," he said. "Melinda, we're all sad about why, but we're sure glad to have Captain Melinda Morris back with us. We's dang proud of you, lady."

Mel blinked to hide the tears his words brought to her eyes. "Well then, I guess I better not go after Hoyt with a ball bat. It would ruin my reputation."

Tom laughed as he stood. "Then I better get to installing."

Chapter Three

Big Brother Hoyt

Tom had proven highly efficient at not only installing the hardware for satellite-based television and internet, but also, he was a wiz at walking Mel through the process of setting up a wireless router and network. Before the dust settled from his truck pulling out of the driveway, Mel had her laptop open on the porch's patio table. She gasped as she looked at the number of emails moldering, having been ignored in the month it had taken her to move from Virginia and settle in at the old family ranch house. She had barely started deleting the junk mail when she saw another truck pull off the distant highway and onto the caliche county road.

Hoyt, she thought, recognizing the faded blue of his twelve-year-old F-250. Both Tom's work truck and Hoyt's farm truck stopped side-by-side, fully blocking the sparsely traveled dirt road. Mel knew they'd have driver's windows down and exchanging the customary "howdy-do's" required of neighbors and friends meeting unexpectedly in the middle of nowhere. She returned to her task of deleting junk mail, knowing she'd have at least a half-hour before the two men completed their visit. She suspected also that she would be the subject of much of the conversation. Hoyt had to know that her response to an unrequested favor could go either way. She smiled to herself, planning her first words to her big brother. She'd have to give him at least a little bit of grief. After all, he was her brother. She and Hoyt settled quickly into the surface animosity hiding their deep love for each other, an affected attitude that they adopted since childhood. Oddly, it had been one of her deepest comforts since coming home. He was still her brother, able to dish out grief while ready to take on all comers if anyone hurt his sister, and she returned the same in spades. They were family, with a closeness enhanced by the continuation of their childhood competition for the biggest piece of pie or who could throw a football the farthest.

Almost all the junk email was deleted, and she'd flagged a number of emails for attention by the time Hoyt's truck pulled into the driveway. He climbed out of the truck, easing the belly he'd developed over the years around the steering wheel. When she first arrived, Mel had teased him, and he'd teased her about being thin. He asked if she needed to open a door or if she could just slip through the crack by the door jam. Mel asked him if he and Susan had decided he needed to take care of the next pregnancy.

"Now don't go making fun of my personal grocery storage facility," he said, patting his ample belly. "I've got a goodly investment in building this resource."

Mel was secretly proud of her brother's quick wit. It kept her on her toes, even if she only had five toes left.

"Hey, Brother," Mel called as she finished shutting down her computer and closing the lid.

Hoyt took a seat across from Mel at the patio

table. "I take it Tom got you hooked up for internet and TV."

"Yep, and it was good to see him."

"He's a fine fella."

"Tom said you already paid for the installation. I owe you."

"I'll take it in trade."

Mel's left eyebrow raised skeptically. "Uh-oh, that could be dangerous. I am not going to pump the septic tank."

"Well, how about helping me move the John Deere from the wheat field on the other side of the west pasture to the one here by the house?" He removed his Franks Farm Supply gi'me cap, and hit his knee playfully with it, creating a light cloud of dust. Mel wasn't sure if the dust came from the cap or the jeans or both. "I already used the sweep plow out west and need to do the field here."

"Sounds like light payment for satellite installation."

"Well now." Hoyt looked toward the clouds in the sky with exaggerated nonchalance. "The alfalfa is ready. Could sure use someone to run the swather while I'm baling."

Mel grinned. "Now that's more like it."

Cap still in hand, he used it to motion toward Mel's metal foot. "Think you can run the clutch with that contraption?"

Mel followed his gaze to her artificial appendage. "Will take a little practice, but I think so."

Hoyt leaned forward, turning his face away from his sister. He cleared his throat, but there was still a raspy note to his voice as he spoke. "Been kinda lonely working the place alone since Pa died."

"You've had hired hands," Mel responded.

Hoyt turned to her, and she could see the glint of the tears he'd hid from her. "Hands ain't family," he said, a hint of anger in his voice.

Mel took her turn to look away, hiding her own pain. "Hoyt, brother dear. My foot wasn't the only thing broken when that bomb went off."

"I know."

The siblings embraced the silence between them, each with their own thoughts.

"You scared us, Sis. You know that?"

"Not surprised."

Hoyt stood up and looked down at her, and Mel knew what was coming. He was just a year older than her, but she remembered too well the big brother lectures he gave as kids and then teenagers, speaking from his infinite older wisdom.

"You may be broke, but you ain't dead."

"Damn right, I'm broken!" she responded. "I lost the Navy, my life with the sea. I lost my wife. I lost my Goddamned foot."

"So what," he responded. "Our daddy was eaten up by cancer but had more life in him as he breathed his last than I see in your eyes now. Our momma done lost most her mind, but she laughs when they start singing down at the nursing home."

"Back off, Brother." Mel closed her eyes and wished she could tell him that every time she gets still, her mind's ear hears the hysterical cries of a little boy covered in his mother's blood, and she cannot remember what she said, what she did. She didn't know the cause of a nameless guilt that haunted her dreams.

"Nope." Hoyt wiped at his face with his shirt

sleeve, not even trying to hide the tears. "I know you, Sis. I see it in your eyes sometimes, the not wanting to go on, but you're a Morris, and we don't give up. I'll just have to keep reminding you of that 'til you remember it for yourself."

Mel stood, facing her brother, not knowing if she was angry or profoundly touched by this man who shared her blood and so much of her personal history. "I remember that simple fact every day of my life. I'm our father's daughter, Hoyt. I'm not giving up."

"Promise?"

Standing silently, Mel stared at her brother, knowing that if she made that promise, there could be no going back, no matter what.

"Promise," she answered.

Hoyt took a long, shuddering breath. He pulled a red grease rag from his back pocket and blew his nose loudly. "Well then, let's go get that tractor."

Chapter Four

Leather Remembers

Mel stood beside the ancient boxcar that had served as the Morris Ranch tack room since long before she was born. The key to the padlock was in her hand, retrieved from the nail on the backside of a railroad tie that served as part of the foundation of a now wheel-less railroad car. Mel felt surprise when she saw the shiny new lock and matching stainless steel key. She'd loved the old padlock with an 1893 date stamped on it. Even as a child, she had felt a connection with her grandfather and great-grandfather every time she used that lock.

Guess the old thing finally gave up the ghost, she thought.

She would have felt silly, explaining to Hoyt why her heart pounded and sweat covered her palms as she gathered the courage to open the door. It was such a small thing in the maelstrom of her current life, but she didn't know if her heart could handle one more grief. It was too fractured and frail to risk it, but she had to know. At some level, it felt like her father stood at her side, patiently waiting for her to do what needed doing.

"Go on, Melinda girl," she could imagine her father saying. "The worrying is worse than the facing."

The memory of that voice comforted her. She

closed her eyes, remembering one of the best days of her life.

⚘⚘⚘⚘

Her father interrupted Mel as she did homework at the kitchen table.

"Get your boots on, girl. You're coming with me," he said.

"But I still have three math problems," she responded. Mel looked to her mother, who stood doing dishes at the sink. It wasn't normal to be so easily freed from her schoolwork.

Her hands still in dishwater, her mother motioned toward the backdoor with her chin. "Homework can wait," she said. "Your father wants some company on an errand."

Mel gathered her books and papers into a neat pile and set them on a side table by the back door. She knew her mother would most likely set the table for dinner in her absence. Mel didn't want to leave her books in the way. The girl moved with swift efficiency, a broad smile on her face. She loved working or running errands with her father.

Her boots were the smallest of those lined up near the backdoor. She slipped them on hurriedly, not even taking time to pull her jean legs out of the boot-tops, giving her a lopsided look as she followed her father out the backdoor and down the steps. His truck was always parked out back; the front driveway and garage were reserved for the Buick that was the family car.

"Where we going?" Mel asked after she was seated in the passenger seat.

"You'll see," her father answered.

They rode in companionable silence. The warmth of the day and the lack of air conditioning in the truck ensured that both windows were down, and Mel played her favorite driving game, holding her flattened hand out the window, feeling the flow of the air around her hand, wondering what it would feel like to be the wing of an airplane. It took nearly a half hour for the drive to town, and she pulled herself up her full height, watching out the window, waiting to see where her father would park—maybe at the feed store for hay, or even better, the farm implement house where she could still get grape or orange sodas in glass bottles from the antique nickel soda machine.

Finally, the truck pulled to a spot in front of the local western wear store with the saddle shop in the back. Mel could barely contain her excitement, as she dismounted from the truck and waited on the sidewalk while her father fed quarters into the parking meter. She loved the smell of leather that filled the air within the whole building. As soon as they were inside, Mel walked directly to the children's boot rack, knowing without looking where those her size could be found. Her father left her to wander around the store while he went directly to the saddle shop. By the time he returned, she'd already examined every possible boot on the rack and still felt comfortable that she liked the ones she had already—not the worn out boots she was wearing but the nearly new ones in the closet at home with fancy stitched red tops and black bottoms and thick leather souls. They were dress boots, the ones she only wore when the family went to a rodeo or when she was riding in the 4-H horse shows, a place where she and her best friend, Addie Romero, were consistently swapping out on first and second place in all the events. Mel was so absorbed in her boot inspection that she didn't hear her father walk up behind her.

"Mel, come on now. There's something I want to show you," her father said.

She put the boot she was inspecting back in its place on the rack and moved double-time to keep up with her father's long strides as he led the way to the saddle shop. She paused briefly as they went through the door to inhale the magnificent scent of quality leather. For no reason Mel could see, both the men working on saddles in progress stopped what they were doing to watch her, the faces of hard-working men going soft as they looked at her with gentle smiles. Her father led her directly to a beauty of a barrel-racing saddle. It had rough-side-out leather, with a seat of red. Arron, the saddle maker, held the custom-made metal stamp with his name and the town where he worked. He put the stamp against a leather strip right behind the cantle, and with three quick strikes with a wooden hammer, the saddle was permanently marked as one of his creations.

"It's all finished, Jim," the saddle-maker said.

"Then I guess it's ready for its new owner," Mel's dad answered.

Mel looked back and forth at the two men. "Who's that?" she asked, feeling a hint at envy for the lucky woman or girl.

Arron laughed, before putting a hand on Mel's head and ruffling her hair. "That would be you, little missy."

All three men laughed

"Mine?" Mel asked, her eyes wide and her mouth

open in shock.

"Well, you keep winning like you been doing at the horse shows, folks need to see you riding a saddle as good as you are," her father said. "It's all paid for, and I already bought a good saddle pad for it." He reached to grab the saddle through the gap between the swells and the front of the seat.

"Can I carry it?" Mel asked.

"It's a long walk to the truck," he said.

"I can do it."

Her father shook his head. "Well then, Melinda girl. You go right ahead."

Even the light weight of a barrel racing saddle was a little tough for Mel to lift it from the saddle-maker's rack, more because she was barely taller than the rack than because of the weight. She managed, glad that her father and Arron both refrained from helping.

That saddle—that beautiful saddle. From that moment on, if Mel ever doubted that she was loved, all she had to do was remember that saddle.

☙ ☙ ❧ ❧

It had been ten years since she had last ridden that saddle. She was on leave, and even Zadab has managed vacation time for them to spend a whole two weeks back on the New Mexico ranch. Before that, every time she visited home, she'd oiled and cleaned the saddle, wishing she had a place to keep it where she lived, but it belonged on the ranch, a piece of herself she'd left behind. A lot could happen in ten years to aging leather in a dry climate. She expected the fenders were curled and likely cracks in the leather.

Taking a deep breath, Mel shoved the key in the lock, then lifted the mechanism that held the door shut. It moved smoothly as she wrestled the heavy door open. She stepped inside, her eyes not yet adjusted to the darkness, until her hand found the chain that hung from the base of one bare bulb hanging from the ceiling. She pulled the chain, and a sparse light filled the interior.

One long saddle rack held all of the Morris family saddles. Hoyt's saddle now rested at the front, nearest the door, followed by a saddle each for Hoyt's three kids. She looked down the rack, spotting the last two saddles—her father's and right beside it, her barrel racing saddle. She walked to it, unable to really determine its condition from a distance. As she reached it, and placed her hand on the leather, she gasped in surprise. Subtle and clean, the leather was in perfect condition. She grasped it by the horn and lifted it slightly. The fleece underneath looked nearly brand new.

The enormity of what she saw took Mel's breath away. She realized that no matter where she went, no matter how far she sailed, her family never forgot her, never stopped loving her. Wordlessly, that love was now apparent in a saddle, a gift from a father long dead.

Mel caressed the leather. She leaned close and inhaled deeply. *Neatsfoot oil*, she thought. *No wonder no mice had touched it. Nothing better than Neatsfoot to soften, preserve, and protect.*

The fear of what she'd find had turned to joy. Mel sighed deeply then walked to turn out the light, step outside, and close the door, replacing the padlock and key as she did so. Once outside, she pulled the cellphone from her back pocket. Looking at the screen, she wandered around the yard until she finally found a sweet spot with three bars of signal. She dialed the number from her address list.

"Hey Hoyt," she said as the call was answered. "Thanks for taking care of my saddle."

"Weren't much. Dad did it until he died. When he cleaned his saddle, he just did yours too. After he went, Sammy and I, we just kept up the practice."

"Speaking of Sammy," Mel said, referring to her youngest nephew. "Do you think he'd mind if I started riding Old Blue?"

"Not at all. You seen that bald-faced sorrel he trained from a colt? Old Blue could use the exercise. Sammy don't ride him no more."

Mel smiled, remembering helping saddle train Old Blue as a colt when she was on leave after Officer Candidate School. The blue roan had made full circle in the life of a ranch horse, from colt, to seasoned cow horse, to old gentle for kids, inexperienced riders, and now, *the family cripple,* she thought.

She had her saddle and a horse. *I've really come home,* she thought.

Chapter Five

Getting Back on the Horse

The whole herd came at a gallop when they detected the sound of sweet feed rattled in a bucket. Mel smiled as she watched the saddle horses become willing prisoners in the corral. She carried the feed bucket to the first of two feeders with large hay racks in the middle and long feed troughs on each side. Carefully dolling out roughly equal proportions, she scattered sweet feed in littles piles on each end of the long troughs, moving to the second feeder for the last of the five servings. They had to be far enough apart that one horse couldn't reach over to steal any of his neighbor's snack.

"Horse'll sell his soul for a half a coffee can of sweet feed," her father used to say. Mel laughed softly as she remembered his gentle voice.

Mel closed the gate between the corral and the open horse pasture. As the horses finished their tasty morsels, they milled around the pen or stuck noses in the empty hay racks, expressing clearly that they noticed no hay followed their sweet feed.

Mel opened a gate to the long run between a set of four larger pens. Moving slowly, she eased up to Old Blue, who looked at her, not with suspicion but with welcome. She pulled the short picking string she'd tucked in her back pocket and slipped it around the blue roan's neck. With very little guidance from the woman, he led easily into the run, and she closed the gate behind him. She was walking back to the pasture gate, intending to return the rest of the horses to the pasture, when she noticed Hoyt's Suburban turn off the highway, raising dust on the county road as he drove toward the ranch headquarters. She paused, wondering why he was in the Suburban instead of his work truck. Postponing releasing the horses, she walked to the gate leading into the next pen, deciding against simply climbing the rails between pens and the yard, as she would have done in the years before. She suspected her metal prosthesis would slip on the rounded pipe rails. Standing in the ranch yard, she waited for her brother's arrival.

When the vehicle turned into the driveway, it became obvious why Hoyt drove the Suburban. The whole family was inside—all except Tom, who was away at college, taking a summer course in forestry. Hoyt stopped beside Mel, and all four vehicle doors opened to deposit the entire Hoyt and Susan Morris clan into the dusty yard.

"This is a pleasant surprise," Mel said.

"When you said you were going riding today, the whole family thought that sounded like a fine idea," Hoyt said

"Wouldn't be because you were worried about your handicapped sister getting into a mess, would it?" Mel smiled.

"Hell, yes..." Hoyt's speech was interrupted when his wife hit him hard on the arm and motioned with her chin toward their two children. "Heck, I mean heck yes, we were just a little worried."

"It's okay, Mom," said Mellie, Mel's namesake. "Dad's just trying to make his sailor sister feel at home." The child nodded her head, apparently certain of her ten-year-old wisdom.

Mel laughed. "Well now, little Mellie, how would that make me feel at home?"

The girl shook her head impatiently. "Well, you swear like a sailor, don't cha? Don't all sailors swear?"

Mel paused to think, considering an honest answer. "Mellie, well, I think I...well, I knew at least a couple who didn't."

"See. I told you, Mom."

Susan directed a motherly glare toward her sister-in-law. "Well, I expect an exception to that trend when in the presence of my children," she said.

Mel took off her wide-brimmed hat, the one that had rested on the hat-rack at the Morris ranch house for twenty years, awaiting Mel's occasional visits. She held it before her, obsequiously.

"Yes ma'am," she responded.

The glare in Susan's eyes converted to a mischievous twinkle, one that was reflected in Mel's gaze as well. The woman stepped forward and enveloped Mel in a bear hug.

"We're so glad you're home." Susan glanced down at Mel's metal foot and ankle. "More or less in one piece."

"I'm glad to have a real home to come to," Mel responded.

"Better than any old ship's cabin?" Susan asked.

"Well..." Mel responded.

"Don't answer that," Hoyt interrupted. "She brought you some goodies, and I don't want to have to haul it all back home if you make her mad."

"Goodies?" Mel asked.

"Yeah, and we get to help you eat 'em," Mellie

said.

"Sounds like a plan," Mel responded.

"Yeah, she even made her specialty," Sammy said.

Mel's eyes widened. "Carrot cake?"

"Yep, carrot cake with cream cheese icing," Susan said. "Now you four get to your riding. I'm fixing lunch and I don't want it to be late 'cause you all aren't back from your walkabout."

"Don't cha mean ride-about?" Hoyt said.

"Whatever," Susan said. She reached into her husband's jeans pocket and pulled out the Suburban keys. Both driver's side doors were still open, and she closed the back one with a flourish before jumping into the driver's seat, starting the vehicle, and driving to park beside the house.

"We got our orders from the boss. Let's get to it," Hoyt announced.

The two kids ran ahead of their father and aunt, making it to the open doors of the boxcar when the adults were still yards away.

"How'd you ever manage to find the perfect wife for my hard-headed brother?" Mel asked as they walked.

"She found me. Looking back, sometimes I wonder if I really had any choice in the matter."

"Shut up," Mel said. "You love that woman to death."

"Well, yeah, but how would she know that if I didn't give her a hard time?"

Mel attempted to execute the behind the back kick to her brother's backside, a gesture which had been their trademark expression of affection since they were children. She'd temporarily forgotten about her metal foot and nearly went face down in the dirt as she lost her balance. Hoyt caught her by the arm and steadied his sister for the heartbeat it took her to regain her balance.

"Dang it to heck!" Hoyt said, grinning. "I can finally win the butt kick competition."

Mel leveled a sideways glare at him. "If you try, I'll tell your wife."

Before Hoyt could respond, Sammy walked past them, carrying two bridles.

"Hold on," Mel said, placing her hand on Sammy's shoulder, stopping his forward momentum. She motioned toward the bridles. "One of those for Old Blue?"

"Yes, Auntie."

"I'll take his," she said. "Your Grandpa would chew us both out if I didn't catch my own horse."

Sammy glanced at her foot. "But I thought I'd just help some. You know."

Mel smiled with pride at her young nephew, and she placed a gentle hand on his cheek. "You're a fine young man, Sammy. I'm proud of you, but I have to learn to do everything for myself. You know, crippled is more a state of mind than any physical handicap."

"Yes, Auntie." Sammy handed her the bridle that was already pre-set to fit the blue roan.

While they talked, ten-year-old Mellie sprinted past and was climbing the five-rail fence like a monkey. She jumped from the top rail into the pen where the majority of the horses were still milling about, not yet giving up their hope of fresh hay.

"I'll win," Mellie called. "I'll catch my horse first."

The adults laughed, but Sammy joined the chase. He crossed the yard and up the fence before the two adults finished laughing.

"They remind me of us, you know," Hoyt said.

"Genetics," Mel responded. She walked with Hoyt the rest of the way to the boxcar. They retrieved four saddles and pads from the rack. They set the saddles outside, balanced upright on the swells and saddle horn to keep any burrs or other undesirable items from being caught in the fleece underside. Hoyt retrieved his big bay's bridle and they set out together toward the corral.

As reality would have it, Mel won the race to catch her horse first. Of course, Old Blue was already in the working ally, and the old horse seemed as eager to be ridden as Mel was to ride. In their haste to be the first, the two younger family members had managed to stir up the four horses in the main pen. Their father reminded them that hurrying to catch a horse was a sure way to slow the process. In time, they all managed to catch their mounts. The horses were very accustomed to the whole process, and were willingly compliant once the youthful energy of the children was contained. As the children led their horses to the hitching posts beside the boxcar, Hoyt opened the gate to the horse pasture, releasing his eldest son's bay horse.

With efficiency, all four of the Morrises groomed and saddled their horses. They led their mounts a few yards then retightened cinches, just as Jim Morris had taught them all. That short walk forced a horse to release the breath they almost always held when the cinch was first tightened. Hoyt and the kids were mounted and ready to go. For Mel, it wasn't that easy.

It did have to be my left foot, Mel thought as she made her third attempt to place the metal substitute into the stirrup, enabling her to lift herself into the saddle. Each time, it slipped free.

"You okay, Auntie?" Sammy asked.

"Yeah," Mel answered, flushed with the exertion and the embarrassment. She took a deep breath, jumped, and managed to get the metal foot in the stirrup just long enough for her to grab the cantle and the horn, pulling herself up, until she flopped like a fish, belly on the saddle. She threw her right leg over and plopped to a seat in the saddle. Gentle as he was, the unexpected commotion left Old Blue wide-eyed and ears perched sideways, expressing his mild concern.

"That was not your most graceful mount," Hoyt said.

"Oh hush, Brother. I'm on, aren't I?"

"Why don't you mount from the right?" Mellie suggested.

"Blue's not trained to it," Mel answered.

"He will be," Sammy said. He stepped down from his yellow sorrel colt. He held one rein of the hackamore on his colt, as he stepped beside Blue's head, placing one hand on the roan's bridle. "Step down, Aunt Mel, but on the right."

Mel did as she was instructed, doing so with relative ease and grace now that her whole foot ma-neuvered in the stirrup. She smiled at Sammy, before re-mounting, her right foot in the stirrup. This time, it was smooth and graceful. They both knew horses, including what was needed to train a horse in a new skill. Five times, Mel dismounted and mounted from the right. Each time, Sammy eased a bit more of his grip on the headstall. By the fifth time, Sammy just stood quietly, his hands at his sides.

"Good idea, kids," Mel said.

"Old Sammy there, he inherited all of Dad's talent, reading a horse's mind," Hoyt said.

"He sure did," Mel said.

Mel did manage to get the prosthesis in the stirrup, but she did so cautiously, placing the toe only. She wasn't sure she'd feel it if her artificial foot and ankle actually went through the stirrup, creating the potential for disaster. They rode together, out of the yard and across the county road. Sammy dismounted when they reached the wire gate leading to the large pasture with a small creek bed, now dry for the rest of the summer, at the far end of the pasture. That had always been a favorite destination of the Morrises if they were out for a pleasure ride. After he remounted, Sammy's young horse began to shake its head and side-step, acting out the way a young horse is prone to do. He pulled it to the side, and while the rest of his family rode at a walk, he loped the young horse in a big circle in one direction, then switching direction for more circles. He kept up the rounds until it was apparent that, as his late grandfather would have said, the young horse had "given up its boogers." After a while, Mellie loped her paint toward her brother, and they switched to a trot, brother and sister riding side-by-side, taking the lead in the ride to the creek.

Hoyt and Mel rode in silence. She was relieved that Hoyt didn't force conversation. At some level, she needed that silence, so that she could fully enjoy the pleasure of a horse beneath her. There was no partnership quite like a horse and rider. Besides, she was adjusting to the subtle differences in gaining balance and a solid seat in the saddle without being able to easily put weight evenly in the two stirrups.

Conversation eventually came. Hoyt pointed

out the new fence he and the boys had erected three years before. The 100-year-old four wire fence that had preserved the southwest boundary of the Morris ranch had finally degenerated beyond repair, replaced by a still gleaming five-wire and t-post, modern version. Their little bits of conversation were about changes on the ranch and in the business of farming and ranching that Mel had missed during her decades away from the family operation. They rode gently through about fifty head of cows and calves, Mel commenting on the absence of the Hereford purebreds her father had always raised. Hoyt explained they developed a mixed breed of Hereford and Longhorn, successfully decreasing their losses from sickness by five percent. Although a small part of the mix, the Longhorn addition greatly improved the immunity strength of the offspring. As he spoke, Mel realized the full extent of Hoyt's joy at having her here to help not just with the work but also to share the burden of understanding and making the decisions to keep the family heritage healthy and vibrant. She didn't tell him then, but she felt relief as a little piece of the void inside her was filled. At no other time in her life had she known this emptiness of living without purpose, without knowing how she could contribute to life. This was yet another brick in the structure of gratitude she felt toward her brother.

By the time they reached the creek, the two kids had found a small pond still holding water from when the creek flowed in spring and early summer. They were taking turns riding their horses through the water, which came to the horses' knees at its deepest point. Sammy had Mellie go first on her well-trained paint. She stopped in the middle, letting the horse drink, and Sammy held his colt at the edge of the water, letting the young horse process through a natural fear. Sensing when the colt was ready, Sammy eased the young animal into the water, until they stood side-by side with Mellie and her paint.

"He does have Papa's hand with the horses," Mel said.

"Before Dad got too sick to ride, Sammy spent every moment he could with his grandpa, learning everything Dad could teach in the time he had."

"Sorry I missed all that," Mel said.

"You were here when it mattered," Hoyt said.

Mel had been at sea, executive officer on a destroyer tender, when her father was diagnosed with cancer. She had come home as soon as she could get emergency leave, able to be at her father's side for the last few weeks of his life.

On the ride back, Mel had begun to find her balance, and she trotted Old Blue, finally easing into a lope. She still felt a little disconcerted and out-of-balance, but she knew that confidence would come with practice and time. As they left the creek, Mel looked longingly along the bank, hoping to see a well-worn trail, one she had made as a child and teenager, riding to meet her best friend, Addie Romero. The trail was overgrown, totally gone, but it still had a place in her heart and her memory. It had always been her "safe space," to the point of feeling magical. No matter where she had traveled over the years, she had lulled herself to sleep countless nights remembering that place, fed by the deep waters of a natural spring, shaded by the massive growth of ancient cottonwood trees. Except to Addie, when they were still kids, she had never confessed that she felt loved by that place, as though she would always be welcome and safe there.

Maybe I'll ride there tomorrow, she thought.

It was close to noon by the time they'd all returned to the headquarters. They rushed a bit to unsaddle, rub down their horses, and release them into the pasture—all but Old Blue. Mel kept him in the pens, planning to ride again the next day. The two kids rushed to the house. They knew Susan had lunch ready, and nobody wanted to miss that.

Mel had been cursed with lack of appetite throughout her recovery. Eating was something she made herself do, but that changed, at least temporarily, as she stepped into the house. This was no ham sandwich lunch. Aromas of tomato and garlic greeted her, along with the scent of fresh bread. Mel fought not to drool, a sensation she hadn't experienced in nearly a year. She was as eager as her niece and nephew to rush to the kitchen counter to admire the carrot cake displayed on her mother's covered cake stand. Sammy looked to see if his mother was watching before lifting the glass lid and sneaking a finger underneath to nab a bit of frosting.

"Uappp," Susan said, using the singular non-word the entire family knew to mean "don't you dare."

Hoyt had paused at the utility sink on the back porch to wash hands and face. He walked into the kitchen, still wiping his hands on the towel left by the sink.

"You kids go wash up for lunch," he said. He popped the towel toward Mel. "That means the big kid too."

"Yes, sir." Mel snapped to attention and gave Hoyt a sharp salute.

"'Bout time my little sister showed me some due

respect."

The kids let Mel wash first, and she had time to look around the kitchen as the young ones washed and prepared for the meal. She opened what had been a nearly empty refrigerator to find it well stocked with milk, eggs, fruit, bacon, yogurt, condiments of all kinds, butter, and pudding cups. The freezer was filled with the white paper wrappings of various meat cuts from the butcher. Cabinets were no different. Canned goods, flour, sugar, spices…Susan had converted her kitchen from a culinary desert to a fully stocked oasis.

"Susan…" Mel started.

"Don't even say it," Susan interrupted. "You're skinny as a rail, and don't you argue with me one bit just 'cause I can see when a body needs a little push and maybe even mothering. Your mama can't do it now—curse that darned Alzheimer's—so you'll just have to settle for me."

Mel looked at the woman, truly her sister even if it was by marriage. She blinked back tears, then wrapped her arms around Susan.

"Thank you, Sis," she whispered.

Susan backed away, trying to hide the tears in her eyes.

"Y'all sit down now." She pointed to the table already set with plates, silverware, and napkins. Two steaming bowls held marinara sauce in one and spaghetti in another. A basket was the source of the wonderful aroma of garlic bread. "Spaghetti's ready, and nobody touches that cake until after you eat lunch."

They sat, and Mellie volunteered to say grace. As the girl's voice expressed her thanks, Mel, for the first time in a long time, found herself adding her own silent gratitude.

Chapter Six

A Special Place

Old Blue didn't even react as Mel pulled herself into the saddle from the right side.

"You're plain old bullet proof," she said to the horse as she patted him on the neck. Blue cocked one ear back, listening.

Not for the first time in her life, she wondered what a horse heard in human speech. She had no clue if they recognized words themselves, or if it was only the tone and the intent they knew, but she did know the deep level of communication that developed between a horse and rider. Perhaps her greatest grief when she left for the Navy was leaving behind Dancer, the bay horse she'd ridden to a state 4-H championship her senior year in high school. Their bond was so deep that she need only think what she wanted next, and Dancer knew and gave all he had. Despite many offers, her father never sold the prize-winning horse that had been his daughter's. Jim Morris rode Dancer himself, until the horse grew too old for the heavy ranch work.

Taking the same path her family had used the day before, Mel dismounted to open the gate, lead Blue through, and then close the wire gate behind him. As a child and young adult, she had loved to ride a challenging horse, but now, still adapting to her physical limitations, she was so grateful for Blue's apparently infinite patience and understanding. By the time she pulled herself into the saddle the second time, both she and Blue behaved as if right-side mounting was the way it was supposed to be. She was even feeling her balance, gaining that sensation of perfect continuity between horse and rider—a feeling that had been second nature to her for the majority of her life. She eased Blue into a lope, making a direct line for a specific spot along the creek. It had been twenty years, but she remembered that spot, occasionally dreaming about it, even more frequently since her injury. The feeling of comfort was like remembering the sight and feel of a gateway to heaven.

They covered ground rapidly. Blue's smooth and steady pace showed that he was still a quality ranch horse. In deference to his age, Mel pulled him to a walk when only half-way to the creek.

"Easy, old man," Mel said as Blue shook his head, obviously having enjoyed the opportunity to feel speed and purpose. "We still have a ways to go."

When they got to the creek bed, Mel noticed again that the well-worn trail she remembered was long gone. She didn't need it. She remembered the way. The cottonwood with the odd branch hanging close to the ground was still there, but it was taller, and the branch actually rested upon the ground. She crossed the dry creek-bed, using the stone surface that made it a great crossing point, even when the creek flowed. On the far side of the creek, she turned upstream, heading for the box canyon with the spring that never went dry, serving as the headwater for the creek. She held Blue to a walk, not so much to rest the older horse, but to fully enjoy the sights and smells she had never forgotten. When she was little, riding her first pony, it was her father she rode beside her first time riding to the spring. As soon as she was old enough to saddle her own horse and open the wire gate, it became her favorite ride, even though the spring was actually on Romero land rather than the Morris ranch. It served as the meeting spot for her and her best friend, Addie Romero. They could be anything they wanted there—scouts for cavalry; traders on the Santa Fe Trail; Princess Leia from Star Wars with the two girls taking turns at being Luke Skywalker or Han Solo. Only at "their" spring were they able to talk about things they didn't feel comfortable sharing with anyone else. If the creek crossing was the gate to heaven, the spring was heaven itself.

Mel dismounted again when she reached the gate at the boundary fence between the two ranches. By the time she climbed aboard Blue for the third time that morning, it felt natural. She was grateful to her nephew for insisting on helping her train Blue for a mounting routine that minimized the use of her artificial foot and ankle. From there, she urged Blue into a lope again, no longer savoring the sights of the trail, now eager to arrive at heaven.

The cottonwoods around the spring were taller, a couple had died, but still remained beautiful in death. Twenty yards across, there was the still cold, deep pool, fed by a spring in the depths below. Mel pulled Blue to a halt and just sat there, drinking in the sight of a place where her soul could rest. Not even the sea had managed to equal the way she felt in this special place. She dismounted, loosened the cinch on her saddle, and pulled hobbles from the horn bag. Once Blue's front legs were hobbled, she removed the bridle and hung it over the saddle horn. The horse immediately lowered his head to lush, spring-fed grass. She considered for a moment stripping down to nothing and diving into the cold water, but there was a long-standing rule among both the Morrises and Romeros. No swimming in the spring by yourself. She could still hear her mother's voice, the last warning before Mel set out to ride alone.

"No swimming in the spring if you're there by yourself," she warned.

"Yes Ma," Mel had answered each time. "Yes Ma," she found herself whispering with no one to hear but Blue.

Mel untied the blanket she'd brought from where it was rolled and tied behind the saddle, then retrieved the horn bag from over the saddle horn. In addition to the hobbles, the bag contained a water bottle and a ham sandwich. Mel planned to "stay a spell," as Hoyt would say.

She walked directly to the old cottonwood where she could still see the initials "MM" and "AR" carved in the bark. Once the blanket was spread, she dropped the bag nearby and lay full length on the blanket, staring up toward the sky, seeing bits of blue through the many leaves and branches. She lay there and remembered, her mind turning to one of the best days of her life.

❧❧❧❧

Mel lay in the green grass, chewing on the tasty stem of one blade she'd pulled free, enjoying both the sight and taste of the greenness of it. She looked up through the leaves and branches, catching glimpses of blue sky. School was far away, and her procrastinated study for a geometry test temporarily forgotten. Ten feet up, Addie lounged on a tree branch, looking for all the world like she was on a comfortable couch, not a lumpy branch with the potential of a nasty fall if she rolled left or right.

"Why do you do that?" Mel asked from the ground below.

"Do what?" Addie asked in return.

"Sit way the heck up there when it's more comfortable down here on the ground."

Addie's head cocked to one side as she contemplated her answer. "The tree sounds different from up here. It's like…like it invited me in for a cup of tea or something."

"Well, get down here. Makes me nervous you perched up there. Besides, you said you had a serious problem you wanted to discuss, and I can't talk serious with you way up there."

Addie sat up, then launched herself off the branch, catching another one with both hands halfway down, just long enough to slow her descent so that she hit the ground with relative ease. Her boots came to rest less than two feet from Mel's head.

"Glad you didn't miss," Mel said.

"I wasn't anywhere close to you," Addie responded.

"Then how come I can see the stitching is coming loose on the sole of your left boot?"

"Is it?" Addie lifted the offending boot off the ground so she could see the stitching more closely. "Yep, it is. Looks like I'll be buying another pair soon."

"Still got some of your 4-H calf sale money?" Mel asked.

"Some. How about you?" Addie gracefully lowered herself to a seat, using the tree trunk as a chair back. Mel sat up and moved so she sat next to her best friend.

"Enough," Mel answered. "Dad makes me put some of it in savings for college."

"Mine too."

Mel threw away the grass stem she'd been chewing and directed a serious stare toward Addie. "I'm dying of curiosity. What's this serious matter you want discussed?"

Addie sighed. "Mel, have you kissed any of the boys yet?"

Mel's eyes widened in surprise. "Well, Lynn Thompson tried once, but I escaped."

"I'm sure you did. You're still the fastest runner, boy or girl, in school, but, well, did you want to escape?"

Mel studied the toes of her boots. "Lynn's a good kid and all, but, well, it just didn't feel right."

"I know what you mean." Addie sighed deeply. "After last week's basketball game, Greg Phillips kissed me when we were out in the parking lot. We were talking while we waited for our folks."

"Greg! Dang, every girl in school thinks he's a super hunk."

Addie sighed even deeper than before. "Mel, it didn't feel like I expected. You know, like it does in the movies. They really seem to like it. All I could think of was I wished he'd chewed spearmint instead of cinnamon gum." She picked up a thin stick and began breaking it into tiny pieces. "I was pretty disappointed."

"That's awful, Addie. I was kinda looking forward to trying it."

Addie held her lower lip between her teeth and appeared to be thinking for a long time.

"Mel?"

"Yeah?"

"Do you think it was because I don't know how?"

"Dang, girl, I don't know." Mel paused to think. "Maybe we should ask Hoyt."

Addie's eyes widened and she pointed at Mel. "Don't you dare. That brother of yours already acts like he wants to kiss me and that would feel just plain wrong."

"Well, what do we do?"

Addie took a long breath, taking just as much time to exhale as inhale. "Maybe...maybe we should practice."

Mel felt her heartbeat quicken. She was shocked at her reaction to the suggestion. "You mean, with each other?"

"Ma always warned me about the hazards of kissing a boy. She never said anything about a girl."

Mel gazed at the still waters of the spring for a long time before answering. "Hoyt said something once about boys kissing boys, and it sounded like that's a bad thing, but I suppose it would be different for girls." She didn't say just how badly she wanted to kiss Addie, now that the subject was broached. She couldn't stop herself from looking at Addie's full lips and wondering how they would feel against hers.

"I think it would be all right," Mel said.

Addie turned full toward Mel, and they looked at each other. Neither one seemed to know what to do next. Finally, Mel reached up, gently touching the side of Addie's face. She leaned toward her friend, and everything changed. The kiss came as naturally as smelling a rose or touching the fine texture of a silk scarf. It also lasted for far longer than either expected, and they were breathless when they finally parted.

"That's what I expected it to feel like," Addie said.

⁂

Mel drifted to sleep, the memory sending her to a gentle place.

⁂

Blue's velvety nose rubbed softly against Mel's face. When that failed to wake his rider, he nuzzled at her eyes and nose with a lip as dexterous as fingers. Mel slowly came to the surface of consciousness, smiling as she did so. She laughed and reached to rub at the helpful horse's jaw.

"Thanks, Blue. I didn't realize horsey breath could be such a wonderful alarm clock."

Mel sat up and Blue took a step back, lowering his head to graze on the lush grass. She shook her head, trying to rid herself of the last of her sleepiness, then she realized the light was odd, even twilightish. She looked at her watch, surprised at what she saw. She'd slept nearly seven hours. At some point she must have felt cold because the blanket she'd originally spread flat was now wrapped around her like a burrito. Thinking of a burrito also made Mel realize she was hungry. She reached for the horn bag, retrieving the sandwich, and dispatching it in the minimal time to bite and chew, following the sandwich with a long drink from her water bottle. She rapidly threw off the blanket, then folded and rolled it, tying it behind the saddle as the unbridled horse stood patiently. She placed the bag over the horn, held in place by the hole sized to go over the saddle horn. She replaced Old Blue's bridle, tightened the cinch, and mounted the gentle horse.

"We'd better get back to the house, Blue. Hoyt will be frantic if he's been trying to call." She patted the horse's neck. "But it looks like I may have found a partial solution to my sleeping problems," she confided.

Blue nickered softly. She felt certain he understood.

Chapter Seven

The VA

The waiting room was about as attractive as a rat in a prom dress. The chairs and tables were mismatched, and the *Outdoorsman* magazine Mel thumbed through was five years old.

Typical VA, she thought but not with rancor. She understood. What money was allocated to the care of veterans tended to go mostly to the care itself. Waiting room furnishings were at the bottom of the needs list. She'd make the same decision if it were hers to make. The room wasn't as crowded as the orthopedic surgeon's waiting room she'd been in that morning. It was just a regular follow-up, and the doctor was pleased with how her leg had healed as well as how she was adapting to the prostheses. Mel didn't totally avoid a medical lecture. Other issues concerned the tired and overworked physician. She turned to the laptop computer displaying Mel's medical records, including the vital signs collected by a nurse that very day.

"Your blood pressure is too low, Captain," the doctor said.

"I know," Mel answered. "And I know you're going to chastise me for not gaining weight."

"So, you're the doctor now?"

"Should I claim that I'm psychic?" Mel asked.

The doctor chuckled, then pulled a chair around

and sat facing Mel. "Captain, you've been through a lot, and I'm amazed at how your determination has you ahead of schedule on the physical therapy, but that won't be worth squat if you don't focus on your general health."

Mel closed her eyes, taking a moment to gather her thoughts. "I know, Doc. I really am working on it, but it's hard to remember to eat regularly." She laughed. "My sister-in-law is on your side. I find a full-sized carrot cake on my kitchen counter at least once a month."

"You eat it?"

"Most of it. Although when my brother comes to the house, he does his fair share, and I'll confess I'm grateful if a neighbor stops by, and I can push some cake and coffee their direction."

"That's good, but a sailor doth not live by cake alone," the doctor added.

"Yeah, like I said, Doc. I'm working on it. So is my sister-in-law. The cake comes with a miraculously re-stocked refrigerator."

The doctor leaned back, studying Mel's face. "How are you sleeping?" the woman asked.

Mel paused for a long time, hoping the doctor didn't notice as she blinked back tears.

"Bingo," Mel said, giving the doctor a wink in a failed effort to lighten the mood.

"I could prescribe—" the doctor started.

"No!" Mel said, in a voice that had made many a sailor snap to attention.

"You have to sleep."

Mel laid her head back, resting it against the wall behind her chair. She sighed as she sought the words to express what she needed.

"Doc, if I suppress what I'm feeling, I'll never remember."

"Suppressed memory?"

"Yeah."

The doctor, hair grayed beyond her years by the work she did, sat silent for some time. "You just stepped outside my area of expertise. Have you scheduled a psych eval?"

"Yeah, this afternoon."

"Busy day."

"It's a long drive from the ranch to Albuquerque. I try to pack as much as possible in one trip."

The doctor stood, walking to the portable table holding the laptop. She typed rapidly.

"I want to see you in six weeks, and you better have gained at least four pounds." She looked over the top of her glasses at her patient. "And not all on carrot cake."

Mel chuckled. "I did drop a hint that I liked chocolate too."

The doctor shook her head but smiled. "Which-ever, just bring me a slice."

"Half a cake okay?"

"I'll make you a deal. Gain the four pounds and my staff and I will take half a cake off your hands."

"That's what I call a good doctor."

That had been in the morning. She'd spent the lunch hour in the hospital cafeteria, forcing herself to eat every bite of a hospital-quality meatloaf special, although she decided to postpone desert for the carrot cake that waited for her at home. She really did love Susan's cake. Now, she waited for her second appointment, with a counselor housed in an auxiliary building adjacent to the main hospital.

Compared to the packed waiting rooms for the various medical specialists in the main building, the counselors' waiting room was almost desolate. She was one of only three patients—an old man, obviously Hispanic, whom Mel pegged as a Korean War vet. He sat quietly reading a book he'd brought, most likely because he had already read the ancient magazine collection; and a young man still sporting a high and tight haircut and the physique of Marine or Special Forces. He fidgeted nervously, staring intently at the exit door. Mel saw all the signs of a man ready to run. She stood and crossed the waiting room to sit unceremoniously in the chair beside the young man.

"Melinda Morris," she said, extending her hand to the young man.

He took the offered hand, and she could feel the clamminess of his palm. "Hank Svenson."

"Good to meet you, Hank. Marine?" she asked.

"Yeah, how'd you guess?"

She chuckled. "They build real Marines from the inside out. Doesn't take a uniform to recognize the signs."

"I am...I was a corporal," the young man said. "Decided not to re-enlist after my last tour." He rubbed his damp palms on the legs of his jeans. "Afghanistan." He turned his full attention to Mel. "How about you?"

"Navy, captain."

The young Marine stood abruptly, standing at attention. Mel noticed he caught himself just in time before he saluted. "Sorry, ma'am. I didn't know."

"Hey, we're both vets now, son. So, sit down, and most people in the civilian world just call me Mel."

"Yes, ma'am," the young man sat, but without dropping the posture of attention. "Respectfully, ma'am." He pointed to her metal foot. "Where'd you get that?"

"Well, actually at Bethesda, but I lost the foot in Iraq."

The old man across the room lowered his book to his lap. "There's always some damn new piece of Hell they send us all to, *es verdad*?"

"Yep, that's right," Mel agreed.

"Where did you serve?" the young Marine asked.

"Vietnam," the man said. "Then I came home to another Hell when people spit on me and my uniform."

He's not as old as he looks, Mel thought. "I'm deeply sorry you had to deal with that."

The old man shrugged. "Me too." He motioned with his head toward the door that led to counseling rooms. "The people here, they helped me. I don't hate any more, and the fears are like small kittens. Once they were lions." He used a piece of paper torn from an ancient magazine as a bookmark and laid the book on the side table beside him. "Now, I still come. They are my friends. I would miss them if I did not come."

"That's a good endorsement," Mel said.

The old man squinted and looked closely at the young Marine. "You have courage, son. I know what it takes to walk through that door"—he pointed to the entrance—"for the first time when you are young and worried that your *compadres* would call you weak. You are lucky this good captain was here to stop you from running." The old man moved his gaze to Mel. "Captain? You look too old to be just a captain."

Mel laughed at the old man's audacity, and she felt more than saw the young man's posture change with anger. "What branch were you?" she asked the old man.

"Army."

"Then you need to change your tone toward the captain here," the Marine said. "She's full-bird, same as any Army colonel."

"A woman?" the old man looked surprised. "Since when did it become possible for a woman to be a colonel?"

Mel didn't feel angry, but she wouldn't let this old man's misogyny go unchecked. "Since the military started thinking with their heads instead of their gonads."

The old man laughed. He stood, favoring his knees as he did so, and gave Mel a fairly passable salute. "I think I would have liked serving with you." Then he sat as slowly as he had stood.

The door leading to the counseling rooms opened, and a gruff-looking middle-aged woman stood in the doorway. "Melinda Morris," she said.

Melinda stood and walked across the room to the older man, offering her hand for a handshake. He took the offered hand, and she spoke softly. "Look after the kid, will you? Don't let him leave."

"Yes, sir," he said with a smile.

Mel didn't correct his mistake. She recognized it as an intended compliment.

It was a short walk down the hallway as Mel followed the woman to a room. The door was open, and a man stood from where he sat in an armchair, welcoming Mel with a smile. He was balding and tad frumpy in a slightly wrinkled green shirt with a blue tie. Mel wondered if he was divorced or widowed and figured he was also color blind.

"Captain Morris, it's a pleasure to meet you," he said. "I'm Will Gold. I've been assigned as your counselor." He motioned for her to take a seat on a small couch positioned near his armchair. The furniture looked somewhat better than the waiting room, and Mel wondered if the counselors were allowed to supplement in their own treatment rooms.

"Good to meet you, Mr. Gold."

"Call me Will."

"Only if you agree to refrain from calling me Captain Morris."

The man laughed as he returned to his seat in the armchair. "Touché. May I call you Melinda?"

"I prefer Mel."

"Mel it is."

He smiled and said nothing. The silence extended uncomfortably. Mel noted the stereotypical, military medical folder laying on the desk in the corner of the room. She pointed toward the file.

"So, am I interesting reading?" she asked.

"Very," he answered. "I'm honored to have such an accomplished and prestigious client."

"Who is currently very broken," Mel responded with a hint of defiance in her voice.

"When dropped, any vase will crack," the counselor responded.

Mel crossed her legs and pointed toward the metal foot visible below the leg of her jeans. "Obviously, this vase was dropped."

"And I don't think the physical injuries are why you're here."

Color blind or not, this guy knows his stuff, Mel thought.

"Bingo again," she said.

"Again?"

"Second time today. I'm gaining real respect for the Albuquerque VA Hospital. Where do we go from here, Doc?"

"I'm not a doctor. Just a counselor."

Mel looked at the man closely. "The old man in the waiting room said the people here turned his fear lions into kittens. Somehow I don't think 'just a counselor' describes what is accomplished here."

Pleased surprise flashed across Will's face. "You have already formed an opinion?"

"A probationary one, yes."

Will leaned back in his chair. "I see right now an accomplished and decorated Naval officer, easily capable of making command decisions."

"Many years of practice," Mel said.

"You have asked me to call you Mel, and I will. Know that within this room, in our work together, it is not the captain I am here to help. It's a woman named Melinda Morris, a woman who has faced horror, severe injury, and, yes, the file also says that you came back from war to learn you no longer had a home and a wife to welcome you."

Mel tried to stop the tears, but they had a mind of their own. "Damn, you cut to the chase."

"Part of how we turn lions into kittens."

"Will."

"Yes?"

Mel's heart rate and respiration increased. "I can't sleep."

"Dreams of the explosion, the injury?"

"Yes and no." Now her hands shook, and she consciously fought to slow her breathing. "I failed at something, something important, and I can't remember what it is."

Will handed her a handy box of tissues. "I'm here to help you in that search."

Chapter Eight

The Plot Thickens

The house was cleaner than it had been since Alfredo Romero's wife had died. Seven years since the 200-year-old home had been fully dusted, mopped, and close to sanitized. He had hired a woman from the church, the Catholic edifice in the town of Littlelake where his family worshipped since the first frame structure was built over a century before. The woman was good, conscientious, and perhaps a bit hopeful that the aging widower might finally seek a second wife. Alfredo had no such plans. His complicated wife had been enough to both love and fear for three lifetimes. He loved her without hesitation, but shame for some of the things she said and did, especially to their daughter, had marred his life. He never doubted that his wife acted out of misguided love, but he couldn't always mitigate the emotional damage to their amazing child. Now, he just wanted peace, spending his final years communing with the land he loved as his father and many preceding Romero fathers had done. Perhaps his greatest grief was not producing a son to carry on that tradition. This day, he had great comfort, despite that regret. Addie was coming home.

Alfredo poured coffee from the aging percolator, one his wife had sworn made the best coffee in the world. He agreed and dreaded the thought of the appliance dying before he did. A short walk down the hallway of the "shotgun" style of the original adobe structure and Alfredo stood in the doorway of a bedroom, Addie's old bedroom. Two cardboard boxes rested on the bed, and he planned to take them both to storage in the attic once he'd finished his coffee. For twenty years, the room remained like a museum display, celebrating the childhood and teenage years of his daughter. Alfredo knew that Addie would, in time, build her own home, but he did not feel right tucking his grown and successful daughter into a teenage shrine during the interim. With the help of the cleaning lady, and a trip to town for new curtains and bedding, the room was more than clean. It had been sanitized of the past—past now stored in two cardboard boxes. He'd let Addie know where they were. She could decide the final fate of the contents. Perhaps, there were even items of collectible financial value. She would know or know how to find out. Addie was good at research.

❧❧❧❧

She'd miss California, sort of at least. For twenty years, it had been her home, the place where she'd successfully built on her three-time wins as World Champion Cowgirl. She used creativity built on a natural talent with a horse that danced on the edge of miraculous. If she'd stayed in New Mexico, her wins would have been little more than an extended fifteen minutes of fame. In California, a place where money was as abundant as New Mexico wind, Adelita (Addie) Romero bartered that fame into a viable business, raising quality horses—primarily Quarter Horses and

Thoroughbreds—including regular sales to wealthy people loving the majesty of the horse but lacking the knowledge and skills. Although having new owners, most horses stayed with Addie's facilities, garnering substantial boarding fees with occasional visits from proud owners who frequently spent their money less for the love of a horse than for basic bragging rights. Those bragging rights for boarders increased after Addie raised and trained the Thoroughbred, Flag 'Em Down, winner of both the Kentucky Derby and the Preakness, coming painfully close to a Triple Crown. Now her top breeding stud, Addie figured she could live on his stud fees alone, if needed.

Raising and selling horses were not her only success. She kept a special string of trained horses and wranglers on staff to provide horses for the movies. She continued to ride and train herself and was thrilled when she was on set, sometimes disguised as a man, to provide a background rider on westerns, historical movies, even a couple of music videos. From the first, her movie business had been a cash cow and an exciting life, but it grew to phenomenal success during her ten years as life partner with movie star Emilia Harris. In all her life, Addie had never ridden any horse that could match the wild ride that had been. Movie openings, rare but passionate times when their work had actually enabled them to spend time together...all of that came to an end over a year ago, when Emilia tearfully admitted she had a new lover, a man this time. She'd met him on set while filming in the Yucatan. The only surprise to Addie was that it had taken ten years to happen. Although a great horsewoman, Addie sucked as an actress. Emilia confessed her indiscretion through tears, but Addie couldn't hide her relief at the news. Emilia left angry, robbed of the power of being the offending party. That fact led to Addie finding the possessions she had in Santa Barbara boxed and stacked in the gatehouse to the upscale community. A blushing and embarrassed security guard told her she wasn't welcome inside. His blush receded as Addie laughed to the point of tears. They'd joked together as he helped her load the boxes into her truck.

Even Addie had been surprised at her reaction to all that drama.

I want to go home, she thought on the drive from Santa Barbara to her own California home. It wasn't the house, the barns, the pastures there that she longed to see. She missed New Mexico. She missed her aging father, and she knew he needed her. She missed…she missed the spring, the only truly magical place she'd found in her whole life.

Addie strained the springs of her office chair as she leaned back, her none-too-clean boots resting on the desktop. She stared out the picture window offering a view of the barns and pastures that were the heart of her empire. Her gaze was out the window, but her mind and heart saw a different sight—a deep blue pool in the midst of semi-arid prairie lands with cottonwood trees around the spring, some as old or older than her family's ranch. It looked so real in her mind's eye that she could hear the rustle of wind through the leaves. A sharp knock on her office door brought her back to the present. She ran her fingers through her short black hair, leaving it in a disarray of spikes. The spattering of gray around her temples remained invisible, quietly hiding by the duplicity she shared with her hair stylist.

"Yo, come in," she called.

A leather-faced cowboy opened the door and strode inside. He dropped to an armchair at the front of the desk. He replicated his boss's posture as he leaned back, placing his own boots on the desk.

"You still sure about this whole thing, Boss?" the man asked. He pulled a cheroot from a shirt pocket. He placed the cigar in his mouth, chewing gently but not lighting. Addie didn't like smoke in her office.

"Sure as rain."

"We got a drought going."

"Okay then, sure as sunshine."

Fred James was more of a spouse to Addie Romero than Emilia Harris had ever been. For fifteen years, he'd served as her right-hand man, and he knew Romero Horses, Inc. as well as the owner herself. Like an old married couple, they could argue and fight yet walk away with no doubt as to the security of their relationship. Addie hadn't told him yet that attorneys were drawing up the papers to make him half-owner of the California operation she'd be leaving in his care.

Fred pulled the cigar from his mouth and stared at the soggy tip. "I guess I understand, Miss Addie. Sometimes Oklahoma still calls my name."

"Just so it's not a call from the Cimarron County Sheriff's Office."

"Ha, ha," the man responded, then put the cigar back in his mouth. "I settled all that up years ago." The cigar rolled as though under its own power from one side of his mouth to the other.

Addie remembered. After all, she'd paid for the damages and got the charges dropped. She decided also to never send Fred to pick up any horses in the vicinity of his old rodeo buddies. For sure the bars in the area never knew of the favor she did for them, but that was okay. She didn't like the idea of her cherished foreman in jail. Besides, he was a settled family man now, and his eldest son was already showing signs of being a master horseman.

A cell phone on the desk chirped mariachi music, and Addie took her boots off the desk and sat up to take the call, looking at the caller ID as she did so.

"*Hola, Papa.* Looking forward to seeing you in a few days." Pause. "My old room is fine." Pause. "You did?" Laughs. "Thank you, Papa, glad I'll have an adult room when I get there." Pause. Addie's face went white. "Are you sure? She's there." Pause. "Dear God, no one told me."

Fred sat up, looking at his boss with concern. "Someone die?"

Addie waved an impatient hand at him and mouthed the word "later."

"I didn't think she'd leave the Navy until she made admiral, but, my God, how awful for her." Pause. "Yes, Papa. I love you too. I'll call later to let you know when to expect me." Pause. "*Bueno* bye."

"What the hell was that about?" Fred asked. He looked at Addie's deathly pale face. "Mel?" he asked, as the best friend who knew all her secrets.

Addie took a deep breath, blinking back tears. Fred had never seen her cry, and she didn't intend to start now.

"She was in Iraq."

"Yeah?"

"A suicide bomber…damn Fred. She's come home, but she's"—Addie cleared her throat before she could continue—"She's broken."

Mel didn't need to knock on the door of her mother's room in the extended care facility. The door was open, and she just walked inside.

"Hey, Mamma. How are you today?"

The old woman stopped rocking back and forth in her favorite recliner, the one the nursing facility allowed the family to bring from home. "Why, it's my sweet little Melinda," she said. Her eyes went soft. "How was school today?"

"Just fine, Mamma." Mel held a bakery box. Inside were two creampuffs, the treat her mother had always requested should any of them head into Albuquerque. "I brought you something."

Mel walked to the dresser in her mother's private room and pulled a handful of tissues from a rectangular box. A small end table rested near her mother's chair, and Mel placed the box on the table, opening it and placing one creampuff on the tissues before handing it to her mother.

"You remembered?" The old woman exclaimed, her eyes sparkling with joy, like an excited child. "But weren't you in school?" Her voice took on a sternness. "You didn't play hooky to go to Albuquerque, did you?"

"No, Mamma. I didn't. It was approved."

Conversation ceased as her mother bit into the creampuff. The old woman closed her eyes, and her face expressed pure ecstasy as she chewed. A small amount of cream escaped the pastry and stuck to the woman's cheek. Mel retrieved another tissue and wiped gently at her mother's face. She knelt beside the chair, waiting patiently for any additional escapist globs of cream filling. The elder Morris looked lovingly at her daughter's face as she continued to savor the pastry. She raised the hand unoccupied by the creampuff and placed the palm against her daughter's cheek.

"Such a lovely girl you've grown to be. You must be breaking all the boys' hearts."

Mel just smiled. "I try not to." Mel's parents had painfully accepted her sexual orientation over the years, but she felt no need to impose that fact on a woman whose mind lived primarily in the distant past.

Marleen Morris finished her treat, licking her fingers for the last of the cream and powdered sugar. She looked to the window, where the shades were open, giving her access to a small piece of the outside world.

"Sun's still high. You going to ride to the spring today?"

Mel looked at that same window. Considering. "Maybe. I'm thinking about camping there sometimes."

"You be careful then," her mother warned. "Addie going with you? Always feel better when Addie meets you at the spring."

A bit flummoxed, Mel paused, seeking an answer that wouldn't be a lie. "Mamma, can you see me camping at the spring without Addie?"

The old woman laughed. "It hard to imagine you doing much of anything without Addie. You two are like potatoes and gravy, never quite the same if there's one without the other."

Mel continued to kneel beside her mother, too stunned to even stand. She realized the deep truth to her mother's words, even after well over two decades since the two girls had been best friends and so much more.

Chapter Nine

A Passel of Trucks

Mel shivered uncontrollably, a cold sweat leaving her feeling sticky and disconcerted. She looked at the digital clock on the nightstand. The number 3:30 glared in red in the darkened room.

Always between three a.m. and four a.m., Mel thought of what had become an almost nightly ritual. She lay there, still seeing the last vision of her dream, the same one she had every night. She saw the eyes of a dying woman, heard the wailing of a distraught child. The dream ended as Mel opened her mouth to speak.

Awake! Awake! Always at that moment, the rest of the dream, the memory lost, swallowed up, replaced by such a huge feeling of failure so heavy that Mel feared it would crush the very heart in her chest.

She lay on her back, silent, even as tears streamed downward from her eyes, and she rolled onto her side to keep them from flowing into her ears. Snot joined the flow of tears, and Mel tried to sniff it back, dreading leaving the warmth of the covers to simply reach for a tissue. She'd slept in a sleeveless t-shirt that night, so she didn't even have the option of a sleeve to deal with the nasal secretions. Finally, she ooched across the bed so that she could reach for the tissue box. She mumbled a quiet "damn" as her hand encountered the empty box, and she pulled the night-stand drawer open, seeking the spare box inside.

Her hand touched not the cardboard of the box, but cold metal—the 9mm pistol. Mel sat up, and did something she hoped no one would ever know, blowing her nose on the tail of her shirt. She stripped from the shirt, throwing it to the floor. As though acting on its own, her right hand reached into the drawer and pulled the 9mm into her lap. Working in concert, her two hands continued their self-motivated motion, and she jacked a shell into the chamber. She stared at the pistol, her thumb on the safety, and she wondered why she did that.

Would the pain truly end? she wondered, staring at the firearm.

"You promised," she heard with her mind's ear. It was Hoyt's voice.

Yeah, I promised, she reminded herself.

Her hands shook, but they were no longer making decisions without her permission. Mel popped the clip, and it fell to the bed covers, followed by the bullet in the chamber as she pulled back the slide, the final bullet falling beside its companions in the clip. She hit the release and the slide slammed forward. She thumbed the safety to "fire," pulling the trigger to hear the snap of the hammer against a shell-less chamber. Mel knew better than to dry fire a pistol, but, in that moment, she needed to hear that futile snap, a reminder of the decision she'd made…that she'd kept her promise. She continued to stare at the pistol, focusing on the end of the barrel.

She fingered the cold of the barrel end. *I wonder what it would taste like.* Would the taste be the same as the smell of the gun oil? It was a smell she'd always loved, ever since her father taught her how to clean her first .22 rifle. *It can't hurt me now. It's empty.*

The hands took control again, and the pistol rose, barrel toward her. It was halfway there when her mind screamed, and she realized what she was doing. She threw the pistol to the opposite side of the bed. *Rehearsal is just a step away from doing,* she thought. Her heart thumped so loud she could hear it, and she realized she was breathing with rapid, shallow breaths. Mel consciously forced herself to breathe deeply and slowly. In time, it worked, her body responding to the effort to regain calm. She threw back the covers, grabbed her prosthesis from where it hung on the bed post, attaching it to her paragraph of a leg, one permanently missing the end to the final sentence.

Clothes from the day before still rested in the chair near the bed, and she dressed quickly then walked to the kitchen, returning to the bedroom holding a gallon plastic bag. She put the pistol, clip, and stray bullet into the bag.

"Sorry, old friend, but I can't have you near me right now," she said to the plastic wrapped weapon.

It was still pitch dark outside on a nearly moonless night. There was a chill in the air as she stepped outside, and she reached back through the door, nabbing a jacket from where it hung on a rack. Decisive action had helped ease the shivering, but she didn't want the cold to start it again. She walked with confident strides, despite the prosthesis, across the yard and to the feed shed inside the old barn. After opening the metal lid to the bin that held Old Blue's equine senior feed, she dropped the plastic bag, carefully sealed to protect the pistol inside, onto the top of the feed there, she pushed the bag to one side, so that she had space to use the one pound coffee can inside to scoop feed into Blue's feed dish. It was early for the morning feed, but she scooped three cans full into the dish, replaced the metal cover, then exited the feed shed through the door to the corrals rather than the exit to the yard.

Blue was alone in the pens now, kept handy for what had become daily rides. She dropped the feed dish where she always did, feeling too drained to retrieve a pitchfork full of hay to complete the morning feeding routine. Trotting happily to his dish, Blue dug in like he was starving, belying his ample belly from his years on good grass. Mel leaned her back against the barn and slid down, the sobs she'd held in for so long erupting like an emotional volcano. She didn't even care that she now sat on equal parts dirt and dried horse manure. Tears flowed and sobs came, and she just didn't care if that was beneath the dignity of a Navy captain. Blue raised his head from the dish, proceeding to do something very un-horse like. He left the feed half-eaten and walked to his friend, his rider. Nuzzling with his soft and dexterous upper lip, he first petted at Mel's hair, then down the side of her face, even wiping away some of her tears. One step closer, and the age-wise horse placed his head gently against Mel's chest. Her sobs eased and she rubbed at the place on Blue's jaw, the place she knew all horses loved.

❧ ❧ ❧ ❧ ❧

They sat on the porch together, the same porch where they'd played marbles when they were kids. Mel pushed her fork through the remains of the massive chunk of chocolate cake Hoyt had brought her from the kitchen. There was no way she could finish it.

Never should have let Hoyt slice the cake, she thought. She sighed and set the remains of her slice on the small patio table between her and her brother. Hoyt was polishing off the last of his equally generous slice. As Mel's plate reached the table, he set his empty dish beside it, and looked intently at the remains of Mel's cake.

"You gonna eat that?" Hoyt asked.

"Hoyt, you need more cake like you need a case of chiggers."

"We're starting baling hay this afternoon. I'll work it off easy."

"Have at it then." Mel pushed her plate closer to Hoyt. He grabbed it and proceeded to demolish what remained.

"You going to bale or swath?" Mel asked.

"No offense, Sis, but you're a little out of practice. I'll do the baling."

"Works for me." She raised her left leg, showing off the boot she was wearing over the prosthesis, a boot that wouldn't slip off the clutch of the tractor as easily as the metal foot would. "Besides, I need to get used to my new foot while driving a tractor."

"Yep, I don't expect your rows will be particularly straight today."

Mel felt pretty ragged, despite going back to sleep after she returned to the house, somewhat refreshed by her sobbing cry and the comfort of a horse. Ragged or not, she'd do her share of the work.

They both looked up as they saw two semi-trailer flatbeds in the distance. The trucks turned off the highway, heading down the county road by the house.

"You order something, Brother?"

"Not for us. They're headed for the Romero headquarters."

Mel stood up for a better look at the trucks. Even in the distance she could see the components of a large metal building on the truck trailers.

"What in the world would Alfredo be building? His house and barns are good."

Hoyt cleared his throat and shuffled nervously. "Well, I ran into Alfredo in town last week, and I got some news."

Mel looked at him, a question expressed in both face and body. "And you're just telling me now? Don't you know you're my only source of local news?"

Hoyt placed the now empty second plate on the table. "Well, I'm not sure how you'll take the news."

"Ahh…nice to know I can instill fear in my big brother."

"Fear, terror…I'm not real sure which one this merits."

"Spill it!" Mel demanded.

He sighed and straightened his shoulders, sitting up straight. "Sis, Addie's coming home." He motioned toward the approaching trucks. "She's building a new barn and pens for the horses she's bringing out from California."

Mel sat stunned. She only closed her mouth when the trucks came barreling by, raising dust that she didn't want to swallow.

"Life just won't slow down, will it?" she said.

"Nope." Hoyt turned in his chair in order to look directly at his sister. "Whatever happened between you and Addie? You were thicker than thieves all your lives until your junior year, then you became arch enemies."

An old sadness made Mel release some of her habitual military posture, and she slouched. She considered going with the old cover story...the whole family thought they'd gone from friends to competitors in athletics, the rodeos, maybe even for the boys. The cover story wasn't needed any more.

"Hoyt."

"Yes'um."

"Addie was my first."

"First what?"

Mel looked at her brother with a half-smile and shook her head in amazement.

The light of realization crossed his face. "Oh," he said. "Ohhh," he continued in surprise. "No wonder she wouldn't go with me to the prom." He paused. "So, I take it there was a lover's quarrel?"

Looking down the road at the retreating trucks, Mel considered how she should answer. "One day we were fine—better than fine. Next day she wanted nothing to do with me. Then I got pissed off, and you know the rest." She reached down to rub her leg. She'd grown accustomed to wearing the prostheses without boots or shoes, and the weight felt funny with the boot over the artificial foot and ankle. "Been over twenty-five years, and I still wonder what happened."

Hoyt stood, picking up the cake plates, preparing to take them inside.

"You won't get an answer today," he said. "Come on, Sis, hay's a waiting, and it's supposed to rain next week."

Chapter Ten

Black Eyes

The rain had come, as predicted. Hoyt and Mel still had forty acres to swath and bale in a field of Timothy grass and alfalfa mix. The cattle and horses would eat well next winter, but the rest of haying would have to wait until the ground and greenery dried some after the rain. When they'd unloaded the first bales, before the rain, they didn't stack high, spreading it out over the barn floor. Neither wanted to risk a fire from the chemical reaction of hay that hadn't cured properly before being jammed into compact stacks. The heat could become incredible as wet hay warmed at the center of the stack.

While she and Hoyt were haying, Mel realized quickly that work was awesome therapy. As she concentrated on swathing straight rows, making it easier for Hoyt to pull the baler, all else was forgotten. It wasn't a particularly intellectual pursuit, but by the end of the day, the depth of concentration combined with the hard work left her wonderfully tired in both body and mind. She'd collapse into bed after dinner, barely taking time for a quick shower, opting not to take the day's dirt with her into a clean bed.

During the break from haying, while they waited for the field to dry, Mel focused on another task. It was one that brought back wonderful memories of time spent working side-by-side with her mother in the family garden. The garden was a mess, fence neglected, including gaps in the wire she knew would be seen as a welcome mat by the resident cottontail and jack rabbits. It took most of a day for her to tighten the chicken wire, including adding new in a section where there was no hope of fixing the mangled wire. Hoyt told her that, while their father was in the hospital, cattle had gotten into the yard and their Hereford bull had ripped out that part of the fence like it was nothing. The big bull made short order of the bean crop. Didn't matter much. The garden was already neglected as their mother stayed at the hospital with her husband. She'd never planted another garden. Mel didn't need to be told that. She already knew because of the dominance of weeds, and the almost total absence of edible plants. The strawberry patch provided the only exception. By some miracle, it had managed to survive, and a few tiny berries were growing on the sickly plants.

Mel finished with the fence the first day, then proceeded to use the gas-powered weed-whacker to do all that it had been created to do. Some of the bigger weeds put up an admirable fight until Mel finally went to the barn to retrieve an axe, before which even the stem of the grandest weed fell in defeat. That had taken two days, the second day ending with Mel setting up a watering system, including two sprinklers, and soaking the dry ground. Today, she finally got to a task she had always loved. She tilled the ground, not with a rototiller but with a digging fork, just as her mother had always done.

"A garden is like a baby," her mother used to say. "You have to touch it and love it if you want to get the best from it."

She loved the smell of the damp earth as she dug up and flipped over great clods of dirt, then breaking the clods into finer soil. She kept finding long and healthy earthworms, knowing they testified to the fertility of the soil. It was too late in the season to plant corn or tomatoes, but she hoped to grow beans of different varieties and the same with squash. This late in the season, she could only hope to raise two of the Three Sisters—squash, beans, and corn—passed down from her family's Cherokee heritage as their vegetable staples. There was time for radishes and lettuce for certain. She planned to keep the whole family in fresh vegetables.

From the garden, she had limited view of the distant highway and the county road near the house. The ancient and rarely used garage and spare room her grandfather had built stood between her and the roads. She neither saw nor heard Hoyt's truck pull into the yard, and she was surprised when both Hoyt and Sammy walked around the old garage. They made directly for the garden where Hoyt had found her working the day before. Mel nearly dropped the digging fork when she saw her nephew. He sported a grand black eye and an impressive split lip. Her confusion doubled as she noted the proud grin on her brother's face.

"What the heck happened to you?" She looked at her watch, then lifted her ball cap to scratch ineffectively at her scalp, an act hampered by thick leather gloves. "Wait! Have I lost track of the days? I thought you were doing two-a-days at summer football practice. Shouldn't you be there?"

Sammy looked at his feet then answered softly,

"I'm suspended from practice for a week."

Mel dropped the fork, then crossed her arms over her chest. "Your daddy's grinning like he just became a grandpa. Your face looks like you had a run in with a truck, and you tell me you're suspended from football practice. Someone better tell me the tale soon or I may die of confusion."

"He got in a fight," Hoyt answered. He looked so proud that Mel was sure he'd have thumbs under his suspenders—if he wore suspenders.

"Who with?" she asked.

"Ferrell Hutch," Sammy answered. He'd quit staring at his feet, and a slight grin threatened to start the lip bleeding again.

"David Hutch's son?" Mel asked.

"Yep," Hoyt said. "The fruit didn't fall far from the tree."

Mel laughed, perhaps the best laugh she'd had in nearly a year. "Did your daddy tell you I was suspended from school for three days after I had a fight with David?"

"Yes, ma'am," Sammy said. "Dad said David caught you behind the gym and tried to force you to kiss him."

"He had more in mind than kissing," Mel said softly. Neither the man nor the boy heard.

"And she hit him so hard he had to be treated for a concussion, and he had to ice his...well...you know, his special soft spot, for a couple of days."

"Got to practice my soccer kick," Mel added. "What caused your fight?"

Hoyt leaned against a gatepost; his grin even wider than before. "He was defending you, Sis."

"What?"

"Aunt Mel, he called you a…a…"

"A dyke," Hoyt said.

"Well," Mel responded, "I am one."

"He said everyone acted like you were a big deal, but his daddy told him you only did well in the Navy 'cause of affirmative action making it easier for women."

Mel laughed. "Coming from the son of a man who joined the Army but was sent home from boot camp and discharged because he couldn't pass the tests, mental or physical."

"That's not all Ferrell said," Sammy added. Mel thought her heart would break as she saw tears in the boy's eyes.

Hoyt's grin disappeared. "Mel, the little shit had to be repeating his daddy's words. He said that someone should put your crippled ass out of its misery." Hoyt pulled out his pocket knife and whittled absently at the gate post. "Might want to watch your back, Sis."

Mel's fury turned her face red, and her eyes became icy blue. She wasn't worried about the threat to her nearly as much as she was that David Hutch's poison had reached out to touch her nephew.

"That's when I hit him," Sammy said.

"Good for you," Mel answered. "But I hate the thought of you fighting to protect me. Sammy, if it comes up again, just tell him that your crippled ass aunt can still take care of herself."

"Oh, I don't think Ferrell will be making the same mistake again," Hoyt said. "Guess what?"

"What?"

The grin had returned. "He had to be treated for a concussion."

The two siblings laughed while Sammy looked on, a stunned expression on his face.

࿐ ࿐ ࿐ ࿐

Hoyt and Sammy left after helping Mel hand till a full half of the ample garden. Her brother invited her into town, to enjoy the evening with the bustle and company of family, but she'd declined. It was the spring she wanted. She didn't even bother to wash off the day's dirt before saddling Blue, loading her camping gear in horn and cantle bags, her sleeping bag and pad tied above the cantle bag along with a one-person backpacking tent.

In the twilight at the spring, she unsaddled Blue, hobbled the older horse, and set him to graze in the ample grass surrounding the spring. She found her favorite spot beneath an ancient cottonwood, setting up the tent in case it rained but opting to set up her bedroll where she could see the night sky, stars twinkling, planets shining, even the distant movement of the occasional satellite passing overhead. She enjoyed the view, but not for long. She slept, glorious sleep.

Mel was totally unaware as a humanoid form rose from the water, soft hair resembling the plants growing beneath the water, creamy skin that varied in hue from green to blue, depending on the naiad's mood or perhaps difference in the reflection of light. The nubile body, perfectly formed, belied her age that went beyond reckoning. Invisible to all those who resonated at the lower frequency of humanity, she walked unashamed, naked as the night itself, as she walked purposely toward the ancient tree. As the naiad reached the tree, she barely glanced at the sleeping woman, instead looking up into the branches where she spotted another being, one with hair of soft leaves and smooth skin nearly the color of the bark of the tree that was her familiar.

"You watch over her this night, my love?" the naiad asked. If any human ears had listened, they would have heard only the gentle sounds of water in motion.

"It has been long since this human has visited us," the sprite answered.

Her words were disguised as the sound of rustling lives. For a moment, Old Blue paused in his grazing, looking towards the tree. He saw no danger and returned to his grassy feast.

The naiad waved her hand only to disappear then reappear on the branch beside the sprite. Both spirits rested with ease in a place and at a height that would have made most people uneasy and fearful. The sprite reached a hand toward her guest, and the naiad moved closer, nestling with her water lily hair against the brown of her companion's shoulder.

"She sleeps well," the naiad said.

"She comes here for that," the sprite answered.

"Was it not yesterday she and another would come here?"

"Yesterday to us, perhaps, but not to these mortals."

As they watched, Mel became restless as she slept. With eyes able to see what mortals could not, both spirits witnessed the darkness of the dream forming in the woman's subconscious mind. The sprite reached forward, sweeping with fingers and hand, brushing away the darkness.

"She will need those memories," the naiad said.

"And she will regain them sooner if she has rest of body and mind."

"Perhaps."

The two spirits sat unmoving, watching the sleeping woman. They were in no hurry. For immortals, there is no need for haste.

꧁꧂

Mel felt better than she had in a long time. For two nights, she'd slept under the stars and the canopy of a grandmother of cottonwoods. Undisturbed, she'd slept through the night, even enjoying pleasant dreams, retaining bits and pieces of the memory of those dreams. No bombs. No weeping child. No unexpected end to a horrific tale. No struggling for a memory that obsessed her with its absence.

The second day, she awoke hungry. She lay for a few moments, at first struggling to remember this sensation that seemed oddly familiar. The granola bars she'd brought were gone in no time. As she licked at the wrappers, she decided that the last of the chocolate cake called from afar. What's more, she knew that today would be a special day. For the first time in over a year, she actually wanted to go to the grocery store.

During his suspension, Sammy drove his rattle-trap 1990 Ford short-bed truck to the ranch, and he and Mel worked side-by-side, planting the garden in record time. When Susan learned of their task, she bought four well-established and glorious tomato plants, each a different variety, and sent them with her son to add to the family project. As Mel gathered her gear from her camp and saddled Blue, she was particularly grateful for her nephew's help. The planting was done, and she could head for the store as soon as she had Blue and her gear squared away. Well, there would be a pause for coffee and cake.

Mel's Malibu made the trip to town in short order. She even played Pink radio on Pandora, something she hadn't had the urge to do since before the bombing. *Amazing what some good sleep can accomplish*, Mel thought. She considered stopping at the auto dealership—the only one in the town of Dallan. Winter would come, or even heavy rain in the summer. Her city car needed replacing, although she was leaning toward an SUV instead of a pickup truck. Her family had those aplenty.

Not this day, she decided. She was on a quest for food. Yeah, there was a new chain grocery store in town, but that's not where she went. She parked beneath the sign for Porter's Grocery, knowing that the fourth generation of Porters had served five generations of Morrises, and she would go nowhere else in her hometown. True, the cart she pushed had a bit of a wobble to it and looked like it was from the same batch her mother had pushed, with a miniature Melinda seated in the integrated child seat. Still, no chain store could compete with the locally grown meat cut and sold by a real butcher, and, as much as possible, fresh produce was truly that, transported directly from field to grocery shelves.

Her early morning passion for food had ebbed slightly, partially because of the sugar dump resulting from her cake and coffee breakfast. Still, she smiled as she pushed the wockety cart along. Thanks to her sister-in-law's contributions, she really didn't need to buy many staples. Her kitchen was well stocked, so she concentrated on the fresh foods. There was beef of all cuts in the freezer at home, but she bought a whole fryer chicken, intending to turn it into a crockpot feast along with onion and potatoes. She was focused on a variety of squashes, striving to decide which would go best with the chicken, when she spotted someone who turned her smile into a frown, but the frown had a twist to it, hinting at a bit of angry pleasure. Standing with his back to her, his plumber's butt there for all to see, was the man whom Mel definitely wished to confront.

Forgetting about the squash, Mel pushed the wockety cart at full speed toward her target. The man heard the squeak and thump of the cart and turned. His face paled as Mel stopped, the front of her cart inches from the man. David Hutch's eyes widened, but his mouth stayed firmly shut as he looked at his high school nemesis.

"Why, David Hutch, long time no see," Mel said.

"You been away," he answered softly.

"Apparently I wasn't forgotten, though. My nephew Sammy tells me your son Ferrell has been passing on your tales about me."

David gulped. The motion was cartoonish in its total lack of subtlety. "You know how boys can be," he said.

Mel's disgust for the man deepened. He was throwing his own son under the bus.

"I know my nephew is a fine boy growing into a fine man. That's how boys should be."

"Now listen, Melinda…"

"I don't think so, David. I think you'll listen instead." The man's mouth shut with a snap. "If I hear again of any of your family harassing any member of my family, I'll be dealing directly with you. You got that?"

David nodded. "Yeah, I got it."

Mel looked pointedly at her metal foot. "Can't kick a soccer ball anymore," she said. "My new foot would slice it wide open."

Mel stared at the man's face, pretending she didn't see how his hands, one holding a loaf of bread and the other a head of lettuce, instinctively moved to protect his crotch.

"Good to hear you're alive," he said, his voice dry. Mel knew he was lying. "Glad to have you home."

"Right, David. I'm sure you are." Her voice dripped sarcasm.

The man scurried away. If he had intended any more shopping, that was forgotten. Mel turned her cart and resumed contemplating squash. *Could this day get any better?* she wondered as she decided on the Mexican *calabacitas*.

Chapter Eleven

Horse Tales

Dust covered just about every inch of Mel. She was grateful for the safety glasses that kept the dirt out of her eyes and the bandana mask that protected her lungs, despite the fact that she looked ready to rob a stagecoach. Hoyt had offered to let her use the bigger of the ranch's two John Deere tractors, the one with a cab, but she had declined. Swathing didn't require the power or precision of baling. He'd offered to switch jobs, but Mel's confidence in her haying abilities was limited not only by an artificial foot and ankle but even more so by her decades away from farming and ranching. Not only did she need to refresh long forgotten tractor skills, but also, farm equipment had changed somewhat in the years she'd been away, another reason she opted for the older, smaller tractor. Besides, the clutch wasn't as sensitive on the old tractor. Working together, she and Hoyt devised a way to put a boot on her prosthesis foot, padding the insides with foam to keep the boot from shifting around, but she would never have the same level of sensitivity she once had to feel when a clutch engaged or disengaged. The boot did more to protect the metal joints of the prosthesis from the grime and dirt of the field. She tried once to ride Blue with it on, but it hampered more than helped her security in the saddle.

She was nearly done swathing the last of the hay
fields, their only purely alfalfa field. The alfalfa plants
were a little too rich to feed horses without mixing
a good amount of grass, so this field was also a cash
crop. The local feed store in Dallan already had dibs
on the majority of their alfalfa, but they'd save back a
few for the dead of winter, supplementing the purely
grass and alfalfa-grass mix bales when both cattle and
horses needed the extra calories to contend with the
cold.

The alfalfa field was near the headquarters house,
and Mel could see the view down the county road even
better than from her front porch. She saw two semi-
trucks pulling high-dollar and oversized horse trailers
as they slowed at the highway and turned down the
county road shared by the Morris and the Romero
ranches. Mel stopped the tractor when she realized
she'd swerved, causing a kink in the row of freshly cut
hay, a kink for which her brother would be cursing
her name as he negotiated with the baler. She put the
tractor in neutral, set the brake, and climbed down
from the seat to stare curiously at the approaching
trucks. She heard more than saw as Hoyt stopped his
own tractor when it was at the nearest point to her
as he followed the trail of neatly cut and lined loose
hay. Mel continued to watch the trucks, not needing
to look to know that her brother saw them as well and
was walking across the field to join her in being what
the local Spanish speakers would call *mitoteros* (nosy
neighbors). Mel glanced over her shoulder to see Hoyt
approaching the barbed-wire fence. She walked to the
fence, grasped the wire second from the top with a
gloved hand and used the boot covering the prosthesis

to push down on the third wire from the bottom. Hoyt climbed easily through the opening she created.

"I'm a thinking Addie's horses are arriving at their new home," Hoyt said.

"I thought the same."

The first of the big trucks drew level to where they watched as it drove down the road, and the driver gave a quick toot of his air horn. The Morris siblings waved in response, still watching both trucks raising the dust on the county road as they continued toward the Romero headquarters.

"Wonder if he's in there?" Mel asked.

"Dang if I know who's driving."

Mel took off the safety glasses, also pulling the bandana off her face so that Hoyt could get the full benefit of her expression. It was the same one she used as a child when she heard her brother say something truly stupid.

"Not the driver, you dufus. I'm talking about the Kentucky Derby winner Addie trained."

Apparently undaunted by his sister's scowl, Hoyt grinned. "Heck yeah. I didn't think of that. Say, what was his name?"

"Flag 'Em Down."

"Yeah, that's right. He won the Preakness too."

"Bet those stud fees are substantial," Mel observed.

"Now that she's home, it should assure the viability of the Romero Ranch."

They both looked up as another vehicle and trailer approached the turnoff at the highway nearly a mile away. Even in the distance, they could tell it was a far fancier rig than anything they had on the ranch. A new pickup truck pulled a two-horse slant trailer. She couldn't see for sure, but Mel was certain the truck was a Chevy. Addie had a loyalty to the brand even when they were in high school.

"That's where Flag 'Em Down must be," Hoyt said. "If he were my horse, I wouldn't trust anyone else to haul him either."

Mel's breath caught in her throat, and her heart beat so rapidly and hard she could hear the thumping in her ears. *Addie,* she thought. She never took her eyes from the truck as it came down the dirt road and slowed to a stop as it drew abreast to where they stood. It was still a good fifty yards between the road and Mel and Hoyt. Mel was glad; she wasn't sure she could speak coherently if a conversation took place. The tinted glass of the driver's side window came down, and a dark-haired woman leaned out, waving happily.

No gray in her hair, Mel thought. It was too far for her to physically observe the golden brown of Addie's eyes, but through the eyes of memory, she saw them just the same.

Addie yelled something Mel couldn't understand, but she did have the presence of mind to return the hearty wave. The window went back up, and the truck—yes, it was a Chevy Silverado—and trailer went on their way. Mel stood slack-jawed, not even noticing the taste of earth from the cloud of dust that drifted toward them from the road. She failed to notice also the long look her brother gave her accompanied by a sly grin.

"We never do get over that first one, do we?" he asked.

Mel's mouth snapped shut and she blushed.

"Oh, shut up!" she said, then turned to walk toward her idling tractor.

※※※※

It was nowhere near the first time she'd come back to the ranch, although when her mother lived, those visits were few and far between. Still, Addie didn't remember any time in her adult life that she'd felt this level of excitement as she neared the turnoff from the paved state highway to the lowly county road leading to the ranch that had been in her family for generations. *You can't go home again*, she thought as she neared that turn with the trailer behind her truck hauling the champion stallion that, more than anything else, assured not only her financial future but the future of the family ranch as well.

"The hell I can't," she said to no one in particular. "My *padre* needs me. The ranch needs me." She paused to reflect before continuing her solitary monologue. "And I need them."

Her thoughts drifted elsewhere, and her mind re-created an image from decades past. She saw a young woman with auburn hair and a stubborn chin. *Mel*, she thought. When they were both in college, home for breaks or summer vacation, occasionally Addie and Mel would see each other whether from a distance as they were out working or just riding on their respective ranches, or sometimes it was closer. After all, Dallan was a small town and any gathering of their recently graduated high school class, whether official or impromptu, would include them both. During those years, they'd achieved an armed truce compared to the competitive battles from their last year and a half in high school. Others probably thought it was because Mel shifted her focus to NROTC, preparing for a military career, while Addie stayed with the rodeo and horse show circuit, a consistent winner in both college team competitions and as an individual rodeo contestant. She'd go on to be the three-time World Champion Cowgirl, a title that carried her to even bigger and better things.

Addie knew better. It wasn't lack of competition that eased the tension. Distant towns and distant colleges removed the daily threat she fought so hard…the threat of still loving Mel and the danger it posed for them both. She never told Mel that, never dared, for to do so would be to let down the wall that held back the love. She never told Mel what happened, what made it dangerous for them to continue to see each other. She pushed that thought away, not wishing to relive the hardest, most terrifying day of her life.

As she neared the turnoff, Addie shook off the threat of a horrific memory and returned to the present. She slowed to make the turn, and as she drove down the county road, she noticed the tractors parked in the Morrises' hay fields. *Yeah, it's hay season,* she thought. As she drove closer, she saw two figures standing beside the closest tractor. She didn't even try to stifle a cry of joy as she realized that one of those figures was Mel herself. As she drew closer, she saw a woman too thin and a slight stoop to the shoulders, unusual for a woman with a lifetime of practice at military bearing.

Dad said she was broken, Addie thought. She pulled to a stop where the road was closest to Mel and Hoyt, the man she now recognized despite the beer belly he'd developed over the years. She rolled down the driver's side window, trying to remember which foot her father said Mel had lost. It was hard to tell because of the distance and seeing that Mel wore not one but a pair of boots. Addie unbuckled the seatbelt and leaned out the window, waving happily. "I'm home, Mel," she called. "I'm really home." She was sure she couldn't be heard, but she dropped her voice to whisper anyway. "If you'll let me, I'll be there for you." She paused. "This time I'll tell you what happened."

Mel returned Addie's wave with equal enthusiasm, and Hoyt gave a less enthusiastic but quite friendly one-handed version.

Addie rolled up the window, fastened the seatbelt, and put the truck into drive. She had a lot to do, including wranglers waiting for her to direct them in unloading and sorting out horses. Mel would have to wait.

Chapter Twelve

Home Again

*I*n her sleeplessness, Addie stared at the blank wall beside her bed. It felt familiar yet odd to sleep in her old bed, as though she, somehow, were still the confused and sometimes combative girl she'd once been. Although grateful for her father's thoughtfulness in converting the room to one better fitting an adult, her too full mind now focused on trying to remember what had hung from that now blank and freshly painted wall. *Was it a poster?* she wondered—something from her fairly long-lived obsession with Melissa Ethridge or Star Trek: Next Generation. It didn't matter, but her brain still obsessed, trying to remember, looking for something to occupy her thoughts as her mind whirled as her old life and her current life collided into one future. She glanced at the nightstand, and she remembered clearly what had rested there for the majority of her teen years, until the horrific day she hid the photo, not daring to leave it visible as a reminder to her mother, a woman she'd grown to fear almost as much as she loved her.

That photo in a cheap metal frame remained one of her prized possessions, now stored among the boxes stacked in one corner of a newly built metal barn and workshop. It was from one of their many 4-H horse shows, back in the day when Addie and

Mel (still called Melinda back then) lived lives so closely intertwined that almost all the moments that mattered to either of them were shared. Addie was on the paint mare with which she started her collection of trophies, buckles, and ribbons, and Melinda atop her bay, the horse that ensured her own collection of awards and mementos. Their horses stood so close that when Melinda's father called out, "Smile, girls," and snapped a picture, the best friends leaned close, arms across each other's shoulders, smiling with joy after a happy day. While Addie knew there had been days equally joyful for her in the decades since, she honestly couldn't say there had ever been one that exceeded the moment of happiness caught in that simple snapshot.

Addie sighed and rolled onto her back, breaking her gaze from not only the empty wall but also the nightstand where her cherished photo had rested for so long. Truth was, that wall wasn't the source of her sleeplessness. She couldn't push away the memory of seeing Mel standing in the field that day. Her heart ached for this woman who, as a girl, had been her first love. The pride and strength she'd always seen in Mel was still there, but Addie couldn't imagine the depths of Hell Mel had known. During the day, Addie sorted horses, inspected newly built barns and corrals— the construction of which she'd supervised from a distance with her father's help—and even settled into her old room in her family's historic home. All of that activity kept her mind occupied and her heart silent. In the dark of the night, the heart claimed its rightful place, bringing to her consciousness what mattered most.

Mel, she thought, just the name. She never believed she'd see that proud and capable woman so broken. She longed to see her again. The bond was still there, and Addie didn't doubt she'd know so much more of Mel's mental, emotional, and physical state just by being with her. With all her being, Addie wished she could wave a hand and free her first love from her pain, her doubts and her horrific memories.

Addie laughed, quietly and without humor, and her mind quested for some occupation to halt the flow of obsession she knew lapped at the floodgates of her mind and her heart. Despite the years, even decades since, Addie remembered the obsession that was Melinda Morris and how the image of the girl, now a woman, rested in her thoughts, only to move unceremoniously to the forefront any time she relaxed, letting those thoughts find their own path. The obsession had lasted for years, her secret throughout college and into the years following on the rodeo circuit. By the time she settled on her own California horse ranch, the obsession only consumed her sporadically, the image of Melinda sometimes waking her in the night, always looking as she had when they were young comrades in adventure. Her most common vision was Mel astride her champion bay gelding and wearing the brown Stetson, her pride and joy her father had bought especially for the horse shows and rodeos. Her braid of auburn hair hung down her back, loose strands flying in a rebellion caused by wind and activity, and a silk scarf tied rakishly around her throat. The best of it all was a devilish smile and a twinkle of mischief directed exclusively toward Addie, her best friend and her secret lover. Those images came less frequently, but they never left, and Addie admitted to herself that Mel had always been the measure she applied to every woman she'd loved, women for whom she never developed the same level of obsession.

A deep sigh marked Addie's decision to put those thoughts aside, even as the image morphed away from young Melinda to the present-day Mel she had seen just that day. Even in the distance and the obvious signs of trauma and pain, Addie still thought Mel a beautiful woman. Addie shook her head and rubbed at her eyes with the heels of her hands. Lying in her old room, she resorted to the substitute for counting sheep which she'd used during her youth. She counted ancestors, envisioning each name in the spidery penmanship of her grandfather, preserved on yellowing paper. They were names which, in turn, had been taken from the fragile and ancient Spanish-language Bible that her grandfather had carefully preserved in a glass case. That case still rested in the family library. The precious and fragile book had never left that case once her grandfather captured all the names, going back eight generations from the very first Romero to ride north from what would become Mexico into the land of *Norteños* in the northern territories of New Spain. Prior to Don Fernando Marquez Romero, the records showed nothing. As a child, where her grandfather first showed her the record of her lineage, she had imagined Don Fernando as a young adventurer who cared so little for his past that he left even the names of his parents behind, starting fresh in a new land.

Lying in her room, in the adobe home, the oldest component of which had housed her family for six of those eight generations, Adelita Romero recited them all in her mind. She silently worked through the litany with which she put herself to sleep so many nights as a child and young adult. She didn't always recall the branches, the aunts and uncles and cousins, but she knew the names of all her direct ancestors, at least the men. On some trunks of her family tree, the mother's name was blank or a single name—like her great-grandmother, Makala. Her grandfather spoke fondly of the Cherokee woman who was his mother and from whom he had learned much about medicinal herbs, knowledge he passed on to his granddaughter, the only one who seemed inclined to learn. He spoke vaguely of how his mother came to marry Estevan Romero, saying only that they met when Estevan went to Indian Territory (present-day Oklahoma) to purchase breeding stock. As a child, she'd taken that answer at face value. In time she grew to wonder if the "breeding stock" were for the horses, cattle, or simply for the man himself to secure a wife. In time, she knew also that the nameless mothers on the family tree were most likely indigenous brides taken by Spanish men. *So be it,* Addie thought, and she chose to believe that each woman had been cherished and loved by their Spanish family, just as Makala had been. She found pride in the jet-black hair and golden-brown eyes she'd inherited from those women. Addie was *mestizaje* (mixed blood) and proud of it.

Don Fernando had been the *alcalde* who led a handful of families to obtain and settle the *Tecolotito* (little owl) Land Grant on the northeastern frontier of Spanish territory. There were still remains of the village on the Romero Ranch, but they had been the only family to survive the disastrous transition from Mexican to U.S. Territory. As the *alcaldes*, the Romeros had more education, and had interacted with American businessmen, even participating as traders on the Santa Fe Trail. The common folk, the ones who lived as their ancestors had done, surviving in a barter economy, still lived largely off the land and the herd animals they shepherded. With shame, Addie's grandfather acknowledged that the family failed in leadership when predators from a cash-based economy, either through purchase or out-and-out trickery, managed to acquire most of the small holdings of the local families. The *alcalde* at the time was young, thrust into leadership when cholera killed his father. Addie never asked her grandfather, for she saw his shame, but she deduced that the young *alcalde* benefitted from collusion with the invaders, ensuring their family's ownership of the largest ranch in the area. The common lands once held in joint ownership through the original land grant were now National Grasslands, much of which were leased by either the Romeros, the Morrises, or their handful of ranching neighbors in an area where ten miles away was still a "neighbor." *So be it*, she thought again. She could not change the past.

As she completed her visualization and mental recitation, back to Fernando Marquez Romero himself, Addie finally drifted to sleep. Still, it was no surprise that during the night, with the coming of the witching hour, her most horrific memory, one she'd buried for over two decades, surfaced and demanded her undivided attention.

❧❧❧❧❧

Addie rode hard across the dry autumn grass. She finished most of her homework during homeroom that day, not letting her friends distract her from the

Broken   115

studies before her. In a different homeroom, Mel did the same. They had plans for the evening. Soon winter would be upon them, and their meetings at the spring would be few and far between as snow made the ground hazardous and the long nights robbed their meetings of essential daylight. She'd noticed her father's pickup was absent from the yard as she saddled her paint mare, but she thought nothing of it. He was out checking fence or the batch of yearling steers in the north pasture. Nor did she think anything of her mother's lack of response as she'd yelled that she was going to the spring, aiming her message toward the kitchen where she assumed her mother was preparing dinner. She didn't even pause to think that she hadn't seen her mother since the evening before when her mother had gone to bed early, pleading a headache.

The paint mare knew the way, knowing also that she'd be hobbled and left to graze beside the bay gelding as their riders did whatever it was that brought them together at this remote spot. At an unspoken signal from her rider, she slowed and stretched out into a slow, gentle lope, one that covered ground but put minimal stress on the horse. Surprise did come as Addie topped a rise and saw her father's pickup parked near the edge of a cliff overhang in the arroyo that housed the spring. She sighed in disappointment, realizing that she and Mel wouldn't have the time alone she so desperately craved. There were reasons for him to be there. The spring was a major source of water for the cattle in that pasture. He was likely taking a head count, including any animals watering at the spring, or sheltering beside the cliff.

Addie pulled her horse to a walk as she approached the truck. It was parked with no one inside, and she looked around for her father. Instead, she saw a sight that so confused her, she had difficulty making sense of it. Her mother sat near the cliff's edge, her father's 30/30 Winchester rifle across her lap. She knew her mother could shoot and shoot well, but it wasn't antelope season.

"Mama, what are you doing?" Addie asked, utterly confused. She dismounted and led her mare toward her mother.

"Waiting for the devil," the woman answered, never bothering to look up, instead staring toward the opposite side of the small canyon, toward where Melinda would soon be riding down the narrow path to the canyon below.

Addie's mouth went dry. Her mother's religious devotion had been a source of contention in her family for as long as she remembered. Even as a small child, Addie had felt a difficult to define fear when her mother spoke so lovingly of her fire-and-brimstone preacher grandfather who had traveled the evangelical circuit of New Mexico and Texas. Young Addie had never admitted aloud to anyone how relieved she was that the man had died before she was born. She felt blessed that her mother was satisfied enough that Addie attended a nearby village Catholic Church, one her family had helped to build.

"I've never seen the devil here, Mama." She licked her lips and swallowed, trying to will moisture to her fear-dry mouth. "If he's coming here, why don't we just go home?"

Her mother stood in a fluid motion, which surprised Addie. It was a youthful movement; one Addie did not suspect her mother could accomplish. The woman took a step toward her daughter, still holding the rifle across her chest.

"Well, I saw her!" her mother yelled. Addie took a frightened step back. She wondered who this woman was with her mother's features but a glow of hate in her.

"What did you see, Mama?"

"The devil, the devil it was, kissing my daughter." She pointed the rifle at Addie, not threateningly but showing direction. "She was kissing you, out behind the barn. I saw her."

"Mama, mama, please don't…"

"I'll do anything to protect you, anything to save your soul. I'll not let you be an abomination. I'll kill that devil if that's what it takes to save you."

As Addie realized what her mother intended to do, her whole body went cold. She shivered in fear. The mare felt the tension, and she raised her head from grazing, her eyes wide, and she snorted in distress.

"Mama, you don't know what you're saying." She reached slowly for the rifle, placing one hand midway up the barrel. "You just…"

Ruth Romero struck with the strength and speed of a snake. The rifle was yanked from Addie's grasp, and she was shocked as her mother laid the rifle butt against the side of Addie's face, knocking her to the ground. She lost her grip on the reins and the mare startled, taking several backward steps, but she didn't bolt. The frightened horse simply stared at her human, torn between the desire to run and loyalty to her person.

As she lay stunned upon the ground, Addie could see Melinda and her gelding appear in the distance, just topping the slope of a gentle hill. Ruth turned from her daughter, jacked a shell into the chamber and raised the rifle, pointing directly at Mel. She waited, and Addie knew her mother was just waiting for Mel to get into range, to make sure the shot rang true. Addie's mind and soul went into overdrive, weighing her options in a handful of heartbeats. Her first instinct was to plea for Mel's life, but she knew her mother. That would only harden the woman's resolve. Could she subdue her mother? Maybe, but she'd seen an almost super strength in her suddenly insane mother, and the proximity to the cliff made it almost certain they'd both go over. Then she knew what to do, although it nearly ripped her heart in half.

"Mama, I see the devil," she said. "You have opened my eyes."

The woman lowered the rifle, turning slowly to her daughter. "But she can still tempt you."

"No, Mama, no. I see clearly. I'll cut her out of my life. I promise." Addie rose from the ground and very slowly approached her mother. "If you shoot her, you'll go to jail. I don't want to live without my mama."

Tears appeared in her mother's eyes. "Do you swear you're saved? Do you swear the devil has lost his hold on you? Do you repent?"

"Yes, Mama. I swear. I repent."

This time, when Addie placed a hand on the rifle, her mother let it go with no struggle. Addie quickly jacked five shells from the magazine, until the rifle was empty. She knelt to retrieve the bullets from the dirt, placing them one by one in her jacket pocket.

"I'm going to lead my mare from the pickup, Mama. Can I drive you back to the house?"

Her mother was now the soft and loving woman she knew. She stepped to Addie and gave her a soft hug.

"I knew God would save you," the woman said. She put a hand on each side of Addie's face. She looked surprised at the rising bruise and small gash on Addie's face. "What on earth happened to your cheek, child?"

"Well…" Addie struggled with how to respond. "My mare, she stumbled, and I fell. I must have hit a rock."

"Let's get you home. We need to clean that and get some ice on it."

Addie looked over her shoulder. Mel was still a quarter mile away and waving. *I can't even tell her,* Addie thought. *They might put Mama away.*

It was a slow drive back to the house. Addie held onto the reins, leading her mare at a trot beside the truck. Despite everything, once home, she took time to ride out the mare, to calm the horse, making big circles mixing lopes, trots, and walks. Despite the worse day of her life, she rode like the champion she would become.

Chapter Thirteen

Return to Sender

Blue was unsaddled, brushed down, and now happily munching on his daily ration of equine senior. Another good ride to the spring had eased the pain of memory that constantly swirled like a freshly stirred stew in Mel's subconscious, even during those times when she successfully focused her conscious thoughts elsewhere.

As she crossed the yard, making for the back door of the house, Mel spotted brown protruding from the edge of the screen door—a manilla envelope. Curiosity made her pick up the pace until she could open the door and pull the envelope free. She saw "To Mel" written in large, block letters on the outside. Below that was handwriting she still recognized, despite the decades since she had last seen it. It was Addie's bold scrawl.

"I should have tried mailing it again, but I lost my courage," it said.

Mel's heart rate increased, and she wasn't sure if it was excitement or fear or both. Despite a wave of high-octane curiosity, she took a deep breath and forced herself to wait to open the mysterious envelope until she was inside, had poured a glass of iced tea, and sat at the kitchen table. She pulled a pocketknife free of her jeans, and slit the flap open, dumping the contents onto the table. Inside was another envelope, a standard #10 envelope, yellow with age but unopened. It was addressed to her. She looked at the date on the postmark, surprised to see the letter had remained unopened but kept safe for over sixteen years. An ink stamp showed a hand pointing at the return address accompanied by "Returned to sender. Undeliverable as addressed." Mel did the math in her head and realized that at the time of the letter, she had been transferred from that FPO address for nearly a year, long past expiration of the forwarding order. Her hands shook ever so slightly as she used her knife to slit open the second envelope. She placed the letter on the table before her and began to read.

My Dear Linda—

Can I still call you that—both "my dear" and "Linda," my pet name for you? Melinda was too "normal." Linda means "beautiful." Yep, that's you, but I guess I've lost the right to that familiarity. I hear they call you Mel now. Perhaps that's best. I still think of you as my Linda, even after so many years. I hope using those words doesn't anger you, so you won't read the rest. I've wanted to explain from the first day I walked away from you. No, not walked away. I pushed away with all my strength of mind, body, and soul. There were times I almost convinced myself that you deserved it. You didn't. Know that pain and grief weren't what I wanted to give you.

I had a good reason, Mel. I really did. I still can't tell you everything, not while Mama's alive. Maybe someday, although by that time, I'll probably be nothing but an unpleasant memory for you. That may be the case already.

I'm sorry, Mel. That's all I can offer right now, an apology for being a ring-tailed asshole. No matter who I meet nor where I go, you'll always have a precious place in my heart.

> *The former asshole,*
> *Addie*

Mel didn't even realize she was crying until a tear dripped off her chin and onto the table. She carefully folded the letter and put it back in the aged envelope then into the larger manilla envelope.

"I always suspected Addie's mother was behind it all," she said to the empty house. "Dad was right. Ruth Romero was bat-shit crazy. Wonder what got into that woman."

⁗⁗⁗⁗⁗

Ruth sat in her car, her forehead resting on the steering wheel, her whole body quivering with emotion. Her hair was a mess, and she had come to town wearing a plain and faded house dress. *My daddy would be so ashamed,* she thought, worrying about a man long dead. His voice lived on in her mind, still ruling her life.

She had slept hardly at all, not after what she saw behind the barn. She was looking for a hen that had escaped the evening ritual of returning to the safety of the coop before dark. The chicken was forgotten as Ruth saw the undeniable evidence of her own daughter and that Morris girl committing an act of abomination. *My daddy would be so ashamed,* she thought again. The recurrence of that thought was no new development.

Despite being distraught, she had accomplished her morning duties, making breakfast for her husband and daughter, starting with the coffee they all loved. Alfredo had been concerned, asking if she was sick.

"Just a headache," she'd responded.

He'd stepped behind her, gently rubbing her shoulders. "I'm so sorry, *querida*. Perhaps you should take some aspirin and lie down. I can finish preparing—"

Ruth turned to glare at him. "I'm not in the mood, Alfredo."

Her husband backed away, recognizing the signs of danger.

Both Alfredo and Addie ate quietly and quickly. They were both accustomed to Ruth's moods. As soon as they could, Alfredo left for the day's work on the ranch, and Addie left for school in her old car, no longer riding the school bus since she got her license. Ruth considered forbidding her from stopping to give Melinda a ride, as Addie did every morning, but Ruth wasn't ready for a confrontation. *They can't do anything at school,* she told herself.

For what felt like an eternity, she watched the clock, waiting for Brother Reynold's office hours at the church. At the stroke of nine a.m., she called, telling him it was an emergency. She needed his pastoral guidance. He told her to come immediately, and that she did. She unplugged the percolator, grabbed her car keys, and headed out the door. Not until she sat in front of the church did she recall that she had committed the sin of dishevelment. Her father, a fire and brimstone preacher himself, had insisted that the women of his household paid due respect to their Lord and to his ordained spokesmen by ensuring their appearance was respectful any time they opened the church doors.

Her forehead still resting on the steering wheel, she breathed a quiet prayer. "I'm sorry, Daddy, but I have to talk with the pastor, and I was too distraught to think about how I looked. Please understand."

She pushed open the heavy door of the Buick and walked rapidly toward the side door to the pastor's office. She knocked.

"Come on in, Sister," a voice said from within.

Brother Reynolds leaned back in his desk chair, which creaked in agony from the weight of his ample body. He didn't even try to hide surprise from his face as he saw the unkempt appearance of one of the leading women in his congregation. The pastor before him had established the policy of sanctioning this solitary woman and forgiving her husband and child for their misguided attendance at a tiny Catholic church near their ranch home. Brother Reynolds quickly endorsed the pragmatic need of this exception. Alfredo Romero was not one of the flock in attendance, but he was in his generous donations.

"Why, Sister Romero, what so troubles you?" He motioned to the chair across from his desk. "Sit down and let me strive to ease your burden."

Ruth sat. Immediately tears appeared in abundance. The pastor grunted as his belly connected with the edge of his desk as he pushed a box of tissues toward his parishioner.

"Why, Sister, this must be a heavy burden indeed. Take your time but tell me your woes."

"Oh, Brother, I fear for my dear Addie's very

soul."

"How so, Sister?"

Ruth sat up, wiping at her eyes and striving for some shred of dignity. "I saw..." She stopped as the words caught in her throat. *Thank you, God, it's not my father I'm confessing to,* she thought.

"Go on, Sister. I am your pastor. You can tell me anything."

She took a deep, shaky breath. "Brother Reynolds, I saw...I saw..."

"Yes? Go on."

"I saw my Addie behind the barn with Melinda Morris."

"Jim and Marleen's girl? The track star?"

"Yes."

The pastor hesitated. He suspected what was to come and dreaded the revelation. "You saw them doing what?"

Ruth wadded a rumpled tissue in each hand and placed her clenched hands on his desk. "Brother, they were...kissing."

"Abomination!" The pastor yelled. "Must our world be damned by these homosexual temptations?"

Heedless of the indiscretion of cluttering the pastor's office, Ruth dropped both tissues on the desk and covered her face with her hands.

"My daddy would be so ashamed," she mumbled.

"As well he should be. You are her mother. You are responsible for shepherding her young soul." The pastor shook his head, expressing vehement negativity. The movement was so pronounced that his ample jowls made a subtle flapping noise.

"What should I do?"

"End it!" He stood, the force of his anger such

that the chair behind him tipped backward with a clatter. "Rid your daughter of that temptation. Do whatever must be done to rid the devil from your home." His voice softened slightly, and he leaned forward, both hands laid flat on the desk. "She need only repent and change her ways to be saved from this evil."

Ruth cowered in her chair, looking for all the world like a dog facing the dreaded rolled newspaper. "But Brother." Her voice quivered in fear. "How do I...?"

"Whatever it takes," he hissed.

The pastor retrieved the fallen chair and reached behind him to the large Bible he used for reference. Color coded tabs marked different subject areas that he frequently drew upon. Any and all possible interpretations of the evil of homosexuality was marked distinctly with red tabs. Over the course of an hour, he read each one to the distraught woman, pausing periodically for boisterous prayers for forgiveness, strength, and guidance.

As she finally walked away, back to the waiting Buick, Ruth felt like a dishrag used too long and wrung too hard, but she also felt a stillness and certainty. She started the car and began the long drive back to the ranch.

"I will save my daughter," she said to God, or perhaps it was to her deceased father. "If it costs me my soul, I will save my daughter."

Chapter Fourteen

Ancient History

The shade of her favorite cottonwood sheltered Mel from the heat of the day. She slept peacefully through the afternoon, a common occurrence these days. As she got more rest, Mel could better recognize the woman she now saw in the mirror. Still too thin, but a few pounds had lessened the hollows in her cheeks and more sleep left her eyes looking less bruised and swollen. The dreams still haunted her when she slept those nights in a warm and comfortable bed, and the niggle of an unexplained guilt still tickled at her constantly, occasionally erupting into moments of despondency, of fear that she would never know its source, a fact that prevented her from addressing whatever failure of omission was its source.

At the spring, she found precious moments of peace, moments shared only with the patient presence of Old Blue. Well, there was the murder of crows who lived at the spring, some of which had become so brazen that they would land only a few feet from her as she ate any food she'd brought to this haven by the clear waters of the spring. Mel had taken to bringing bags of birdseed, scattering handfuls toward the waiting birds, a practice that brought them ever closer. She enjoyed their caws of welcome when she arrived, and she wondered how they knew to leave her in peace as she settled in for a nap or for a night's sleep at her campsite when she slept under the ancient cottonwood.

Today, the nap routine would change. Mel awoke as Old Blue raised his head from grazing, his ears perked forward in rapt attention. He called the clear and simple message of one horse greeting another, and despite his hobbles, he managed to move with surprising speed to the far side of the meadow. Mel sat up abruptly from her saddle pillow, rubbing at her eyes. A second horse could be heard returning the greeting from somewhere just over the ridge at the top of the small canyon. Mel stood a tad shakily, striving to recover from her deep sleep. As she watched, she saw a blood bay top the ridge, and, for a moment, she felt a dizzying time warp, as though nearly three decades had never happened.

Addie sat atop the beautiful bay gelding. Her Addie was back, back at their private meeting place.

"Surprise, surprise!" Addie called.

"That's an understatement."

Addie urged the gelding into a trot as they descended the path into the canyon, crossing the last twenty yards with ease. She pulled him to a slow walk as they neared Mel. Old Blue nickered another welcome, as he made his way toward Addie and her mount. Both women watched unperturbed as the two horses snuffled and smelled, getting to know each other. Addie dismounted and the two women stood facing each other. Mel had no clue what to say next, and Addie, a woman rarely speechless, stood with her mouth slightly open, as if in preparation of speech, but no words came.

"This is…strange," Mel finally said.

"It's been a long time since we were at the spring together."

Mel was surprised to feel the sting of pending tears. "There's no bridge here, but if there were, there would be a lot of water under it."

Addie chuckled. "You always have a joke for those awkward moments."

"Better than silence."

"I need to tell you something," Addie said.

"I suspect we have a thousand things to tell each other."

Addie reached out and placed a hand on Mel's arm. The touch caused a reaction so intense for Mel that she equated it with an electric shock, although much more pleasant.

"Mel, this has to come first, and it's big. Not sure I can look at you while I explain something, something I couldn't say nearly thirty years ago."

"Then let's sit," Mel said. She motioned toward the saddle and horn bag resting on the ground where she'd slept. "I have some tea left in the thermos, but we'll have to share a cup." At that statement, Addie glanced at her with an intensity that surprised them both.

"I kinda like that thought," Addie said.

Mel blushed but said nothing, instead turning to her kit on the ground, bending to pull the thermos from the horn bag. At the same time, Addie led the bay to a low hanging branch on the cottonwood and tied him to it, using the lead from the halter he wore under his bridle. She threw the reins over his neck and tied them in a loose knot just below his chin. Mel was already seated, her back to the trunk of the tree, and Addie moved to take a seat beside her. Neither seemed to notice that she sat close enough for their arms to touch. It felt so natural that it was done without thought. Mel handed Addie the still steaming cup of tea.

"Sweet, like you like it," Addie said as she took a sip.

"Some things don't change."

"And some things do," Addie responded. She looked at Mel, regret so obvious in her eyes that the look alone took Mel's breath away. "Mama's dead, Mel. I don't have to keep a horrible secret any longer, at least not from you, and you're the one who matters."

"A secret?"

Addie took a deep breath and Mel noticed a ripple in the dark tea in the cup. Addie's hand was shaking. Mel took the cup from her, took a long drink and then set it on the ground beside the tree trunk.

"Then tell. I'll listen," Mel said.

Addie looked everywhere except at Mel as the tale unfolded. A story told just yards from where it happened but a distance of decades between the living and the telling. She told of her mother's obsession, of the rifle, of the steps her teenaged self believed were the only way to save the life of the girl who was her love. She didn't say her next thought. *The one I've always loved.*

Mel felt caught in a time warp as the biggest mystery of her life was finally understood. The pain and anger she'd felt as a youth when the most important person in her life had turned against her, transforming overnight from lover and friend to nemesis evolved into gratitude as she realized how close she'd come to an ended life before it had fully begun.

From not being able to look at Mel as she told

the story, Addie now stared at the other woman with rapt attention, obviously waiting for a reaction. As the silence continued, her breathing grew shallow and her pupils dilated with emotion.

"You saved my life," Mel finally said.

"And then I made it miserable. I'm so sorry."

"You were very convincing," Mel said.

"Only because I worked so hard to convince myself...that it was all your fault, that you seduced me. Took me forever to come to terms with being gay." She looked quizzically at Mel. "When did you know, without a doubt?"

Mel chuckled. "Sitting right here in the shade of this very tree, that first time we kissed."

"In time, we did a whole lot more." Addie dropped her gaze, staring at her boot toes. "I worked hard to convince myself that it was all your fault."

"Uh, as I recall, you kissed me first."

Addie blushed. "Yeah, I tried not to remember that back then."

"And now?"

Addie reached up to touch Mel's cheek. "I remember it fondly."

"Me too." A mischievous sparkle gave new life to eyes dulled for too long by pain, injury, and the memory of a living nightmare. "So."

"So what?"

"You could do it again." A hint of doubt lessened the sparkle. "If you wanted to, that is."

Addie laughed gently before placing her free hand on Mel's other cheek, gently holding the injured woman's face. There was no need. Mel didn't wait. She was the one to lean toward Addie and initiate a kiss delayed by nearly thirty years. The kiss went on and on, remaining gentle, for it was more of healing than of passion. In time, they moved away from the rough bark of the tree to lay in each other's arms. In time, the kisses stopped but not the loving. Addie rolled onto her back, and Mel rested her head on Addie's shoulder, each woman simply enjoying the physical presence of the other.

"It haunts me, Addie."

Addie said nothing, she tightened the embrace, using one hand to brush a wisp of hair from Mel's face. She waited silently, just as she waited patiently to gain the trust of a young horse. Slowly, painfully, Mel told of that day, that awful day, in more detail than she'd ever shared, even with the VA therapists who sought to help her. Addie listened. She blinked back tears and lay as still as possible, striving to give Mel the safety and comfort she needed to relive those moments in Hell. Mel stopped as she told of looking in the eyes of a dying mother.

The silence went on until Addie finally whispered, "You don't have to tell me the rest now, love. Only when you're ready."

"I would." Mel lifted herself, leaning on one elbow, looking intensely at the woman beside her. "Addie, I can't remember."

"You probably passed out."

"No, no. I did something wrong, but I can't remember."

"Honey, you didn't do anything wrong. The world did something wrong. There never should be a place where parents can't enjoy moments with their child in a quiet café without fear of a bomb."

Mel sat up, her hand over her mouth as her respiration quickened. "No, you don't understand. I know I did something wrong."

Addie sat up too, putting her arms around Mel, holding her from behind. "Whatever it is, you'll remember when the time is right." She kissed Mel's neck. "And you won't have to face it alone."

Mel held Addie's arms where they crossed her own chest. "I know."

Abruptly, Mel stood and walked to the edge of the water at the spring. She knelt there and used both hands to splash cold water onto her reddened and tear streaked face.

"God, don't I look great for a reunion?"

"I think having you near me, beside me, is the most beautiful sight I've ever seen."

Mel stood and faced Addie, who now sat, her back once again against the truck of the tree. "I feel the same about you."

She looked to the sun as it dropped closer to the horizon. "I hate to end this, but we both need to leave unless we want to ride home in the dark."

Mel walked toward her saddle and other tack. She retrieved the bridle from under the saddle, and walked toward Old Blue, who patiently waited, opening his mouth to accept the bit. By the time she'd removed the hobbles and led him back to her saddle, Addie already had the saddle and pad ready to place on Old Blue's back. Working together, the two horsewomen had Blue saddled and ready to ride in a short time. It was as if no time had passed since the last time they worked together saddling a horse. Addie walked to her bay gelding, untying his halter, and tying the lead loosely to the saddle horn. She led the bay toward Mel and Old Blue, pausing in surprise as she watched Mel mount from the right.

"When did you start doing that?" Addie asked.

"Mounting from the wrong side?"

"Yep."

"Since I grew a metal foot that slips out of the stirrup if I use it to lift myself into the saddle."

"Makes sense."

Addie watched as Mel put the prosthesis into the stirrup, accidentally slipping the entire contraption through the open stirrup. Leading the gelding, Addie stepped to the side of Old Blue, and grasped the stirrup and metal foot, freeing the artificial appendage and placing it safely just into the stirrup.

"That's dangerous," Addie said. "You need tapaderos."

"I know. Looked for them in Albuquerque. All they had was either the big huge fancy ones or the little ones that go on pony saddles. I'll keep looking."

Addie frowned. "Sooner better than later. If you came off, even if your horse just stumbled, you could be drug to death."

"On Blue? Most bullet proof horse I've ever ridden."

"Even good horses can get in big messes."

Mel laughed heartily. "Do you realize you just quoted my father?"

"He was right."

Addie mounted her horse effortlessly. The young gelding wasn't as amicable to the closeness as the horses the two girls had ridden decades before, but they still managed to maneuver their mounts so that they could exchange a goodbye kiss.

"Want to ride home with me tonight?" Addie asked.

"I wish," Mel responded. "We got a sick steer in

the pens. I need to feed and check on him."

"Tomorrow?" Addie asked.

"Wild horses couldn't keep me away."

"Well, can they bring you instead? I'll be working on halter training a couple of colts."

Mel laughed. "Old times all over again."

"God, I hope so," Addie said before turning her gelding and giving him his head. They headed up the trail to the canyon rim at a lope.

Mel watched, entranced. For the first time in a long time, she had a moment of utter happiness.

Chapter Fifteen

Unexpected Memories

As promised, Mel arrived at the Romero Ranch headquarters in time to join Addie and her father at the breakfast table. She paused at the kitchen door—the "servants' entrance." Throughout her childhood, she never remembered entering through the front door, always the kitchen door and frequently without knocking first. Addie and Melinda would rush in, disheveled and sweaty from their latest horseback adventure, gulp down iced tea or soda, then rush off to Addie's room to play board games or to simply giggle and talk.

Mel paused as she considered the door, noting it was the same door, although now red instead of the white she'd always known. Her absence was now so long in the past that the red showed cracks and fading from years of age. Mel smiled, thinking of the long-neglected front door. Alfredo used to joke that a knock from that door was a sure sign of a salesman, a politician, or a Jehovah's Witness.

Mel raised her fist to knock. The door opened abruptly, and Mel barely managed to pull back in time to avoid a hard tap to Addie's forehead as the women stood in the now open doorway.

"We were starting to wonder if you were ever coming inside," Addie said.

"I was admiring the red door."

Addie glanced at the door, still white on the inside. "Good God, has it really been that long since you were here? We painted it red when I was in college." Her eyes scrunched up as she rummaged through neglected memory files. "I think it was ten or eleven years ago Dad finally repainted."

Mel was amazed at how comfortable she felt as Alfredo motioned toward the coffee pot, and Mel took a cup from the cabinet where they had always been, poured coffee from the same percolator Addie's mother, Ruth, had used so many years before. As a girl, Mel had secretly wondered how a woman so sour could make coffee and food that tasted so full of love. She couldn't have expressed it as a child, but Mel now realized the term "comfort food" took on a whole new meaning for Addie. Food—good food, healthy food—had been the only way Ruth could comfortably express love. Well, not the only way. Preaching for the salvation of their rebellious young souls had been an aggravating but well-intended expression of love. Luckily, Alfredo's secret eye-rolls and Mel's parents' sighs and comments of "that Ruth" had done much to prevent any permanent damage to the confidence and sense of self-worth for Mel. As an adult, she realized Addie hadn't been quite so lucky. Understandable. Ruth was her mother, not Mel's.

As she put milk and sugar in the freshly poured coffee—assuming as she did so that Alfredo's coffee would be as strong as that his late wife made—Mel's mind returned to the present. She took a seat at the table, sitting in the same spot she'd always taken as a child. She noticed the absence of the 1950s vintage Formica table and padded chrome chairs, replaced by a serviceable wooden version.

"Good to see you, Melinda," Alfredo said.

"More than pleased to see you, Mr. Romero."

Alfredo chuckled. "Mr. Romero? You're a grown woman now, Melinda." He reached across the table and patted her hand. "And you are still like a second daughter to me. You can call me Papa if you want, but I'd prefer Alfredo."

Melinda blinked back tears. "Alfredo it is," she said.

The man smiled and returned to reading the morning news from an iPad, another change Mel acknowledged. As a child, she and Addie had enough sleepovers that Mel had seen Alfredo at the breakfast table with some newspaper or another at every visit. Back then, the news was frequently a week old before it made it to the ranch, but Alfredo always kept up with current events through *The Albuquerque Journal*, the *Santa Fean*, and *The Wall Street Journal*.

Some things change, and some things don't, Mel thought.

"Had breakfast?" Addie asked. She then took the last bite of bacon from a decimated plate of bacon and eggs.

"Yep, a slice of Sally's carrot cake."

"How healthy is that?"

"Very healthy when you're on doctor's orders to gain weight."

Alfredo glanced up from his iPad. "I wasn't going to say anything, but I am planning to make you girls a good lunch. Stuffed sopapillas okay?"

Mel glanced at the man in surprise. "You cook?"

"No, I've starved to death since my wife died. What you see is a ghost," he said with a totally straight face.

Mel had forgotten Alfredo's droll humor. She laughed. "Stuffed sopapillas sound great. Love 'em but they weren't a part of the officer's mess at any command I experienced."

"Was the food good in the Navy?" Addie asked.

"Sometimes, but mostly it was hot and welcome because the work was hard." Mel raised her coffee cup. "Our mothers prepared me well for the Navy 'cause the coffee was always strong enough to clean a carburetor."

Addie and Alfredo chuckled. "Your mom called it cowboy coffee," Addie said.

Alfredo smiled and pointed a finger at his daughter. "And your mother just called it coffee."

"You bet. Don't remember ever going out to eat with her that she didn't complain about the coffee being nothing but dirty dish water," Addie said.

"At the Cowboy Café in Slader, I think it was," Mel added.

"Was what?" Addie asked.

"Dirty dishwater. Damn, that was nasty stuff. I hear the café there closed."

"Twenty years ago," Alfredo said. "The only thing good there was blueberry pie, and that wasn't enough to keep it open."

"What happened to the big, plaster, bow-legged cowboy that stood over the front entrance?"

"Some trendy restaurant in Clovis bought it and fixed it up. Went there once when I was there for a horse show. Cowboy looks better and the food is a heckuva lot better. No blueberry pie though," Addie said.

Mel rubbed her chin thoughtfully. "Hmm...I

used to make good pie."

"You won a couple of ribbons in 4-H for your pie," Addie said.

"I may have to revive blueberry pie just for you two."

Alfredo's eyes twinkled. "I knew there was a reason I loved you like a second daughter."

Addie finished her last bite of toast, gulped the last of her coffee, then headed to the sink with her dishes. "Mel, you finished with your coffee?"

Mel looked into her half-full mug. "I guess so," she answered, directing a wink at Alfredo.

"Leave the dishes. I'll do those," Alfredo said.

"We got chores and two yearlings needing halter training. Let's go," Addie said, both hands on her hips in an impatient posture.

Some things change, and some things don't, Mel thought as she rose from her chair, a lopsided smile on her face.

"What you grinning at?"

"You," Mel answered. "Amazed at how much I've missed your bossiness."

Alfredo rose from his chair and belly laughed as he crossed the kitchen, carrying his own plate, cup, and cutlery to the sink.

※ ※ ※ ※

Chores had been easy. New additions to the Romero property included two high-end single-wide trailers, now occupied by a young couple, both experienced horse people, in one and an older cowboy who walked with a limp in the other. The limp came from the greenstick fracture when his foot caught in the stirrup of a saddle-bronc, permanently ending his rodeo career. Addie saw the accident and visited the cowboy in the hospital, then offered him a job even before he was out of a cast. It had been a wise move for both. He worked with the horses he loved, and Addie found a mature, dependable hand. The hands did most of the feeding of the horses and were beginning to help around the existing cattle ranch as well.

Still, Addie herself fed, checked, and groomed the stallion who was the cornerstone of her business. When, as a three-year-old, Flag 'Em Down won two of the most prestigious races, he earned a life of coital bliss for himself, and huge stud fees for his owner. At present, there were three mares in the section of the barn and corrals specifically designated for the stud's visiting harem. One was confirmed pregnant and the other two were waiting on a vet's visit. Addie already knew they were with foal based on their behavior, but she needed that veterinarian confirmation before sending the mares back to their owners.

Addie had her own herd of seven broodmares, all Quarter Horses, but she didn't keep a stud for them. Those she sent out to top notch Quarter Horse stallions for the same service her champion Thoroughbred provided for others. Knowing the move was pending, she kept her beautiful mares celibate for the year, but she had started the weaning and training process for two of the yearlings—one colt and one filly—now ready for the separation from their mamas. It was those two little troublemakers for which she now recruited Mel's assistance. The two youngsters and their mamas were over the worst of the weaning angst, and both Addie and Maria— the wife of the young couple among the permanent hands—were taking time each day to handle and play with the yearlings. It was a pleasure more than a job, causing an increased bonding between Addie and her helper as they shared laughter at the young horses' antics. The rubber chicken episode was becoming legendary after the filly discovered it squeaked if she shook it up and down while holding it in her mouth. The colt had not liked the obnoxious noise, so the filly chased her playmate, chicken fully vocalized, around the pen. The two women laughed until Maria fell to the ground and Addie was wiping tears from her eyes. After a half hour, Addie started to worry the young male might be permanently traumatized. She then proved Jim Morris' old adage that a horse would sell its soul for half a coffee can of sweet feed. The filly dropped the chicken immediately once she heard the rattle of grain in a metal bucket. Marie nabbed the chicken while Addie poured grain into each of the yearlings' feed bins.

Today would not be all fun and games. It was time to introduce the young horses to the concept of a halter. Addie knew she and Maria could handle the process, but she had more on her mind than the training of young horses. Mel wasn't a quitter, never had been, but she was broken, and Addie knew the healing power of horses. Old Blue was obviously a lifeline for the Navy veteran, but Mel was a woman accustomed to adventure, to challenges. When they were girls, Addie had never seen a horse that could frighten Mel, and Mel had a touch, a way with horses that almost rivaled her late father. In all her years raising and training horses, Addie had never seen that level of magic anywhere else, and she was grateful that her skills had the opportunity to develop under the guidance of Jim Morris, the horse whisperer himself.

Mel helped Addie feed and brush down Flag 'Em Down (affectionately referred to as Flaggy) before they turned their attention to the yearlings. The three permanent hired hands were busy around the barns, feeding and checking water in the troughs. Addie introduced Mel to all her employees, and Mel was pleased to see that all her successes hadn't touched Addie's basic sense of human decency. No atmosphere of boss and hireling marred the introductions.

The humans were forgotten as Addie opened the gate, and the two women entered the pen where the yearlings waited. As instructed, Joe Bob placed grain and hay for the two foals in their stalls in the barn. The yearlings were munching breakfast as Addie entered the colt's stall and Mel the filly's. Each woman had a yearling-sized halter discretely tucked in their back pockets. They started petting the young horses as they ate, working in their own ways and at their own speed; they went from petting with hands to rubbing each young horse with the halter they eased out of their pockets. So carefully was it done that neither horse reacted. Addie had progressed to rubbing the colt along the neck and chest when she saw Mel leaning on the fence between the two stalls, watching Addie as she worked.

"I thought you were going to put the halter on the filly?" Addie asked.

"Done," Mel answered.

"You stinker," Addie said. "Just showing off."

"Yep, haven't lost my touch."

The colt heard the change in vocal tone and raised his head from the feed momentarily. Addie eased the halter back into her pocket, and slowly stepped out of the stall. She watched the filly eating her breakfast, apparently unaware that she now wore a halter. Addie pulled the halter from her pocket and held it toward Mel.

"Well then, show off some more and do the other one."

Mel smiled mischievously. "You're the boss." She took the halter, eased into the stall, speaking softly to the young horse. "Good breakfast, young fella? Mine was good this morning too, especially the coffee when I got here. Too bad the boss lady wouldn't let me finish."

Mel looked at Addie and winked. Addie smiled, even as she wagged a finger toward Mel in playful admonition. Mel continued to talk nonsense in a soft voice, telling the young horse all about her carrot cake breakfast, and the color of the sunrise as she left the house to drive here. One horsey ear swiveled her direction, as though he wanted to hear every word. Mel rubbed the halter all over the young horse, even leaning across his back to reach the far side. She went up his neck, using her other hand to rub along the side of his face. As she watched, Addie remembered when Jim Morris had shown both the girls that special spot on a horse's jaw that calmed the animal, sometimes like a magic button. The colt paused chewing for a minute, releasing a deep, relaxed sigh. Mel reached over the horse's neck, halter bunched in her hand, and rubbed the magic spot on the opposite jaw. With her other hand, Mel rubbed along the colt's face, even his soft nose. For a moment, the colt's eyes widened as she felt slowly and gently all around the nose and mouth, speaking soft nonsense the whole time; in moments, the colt relaxed, grabbing another mouthful of grain.

The young horse didn't even react when the halter replaced the human touch. In a seamless movement, Mel latched the buckle on the halter, still rubbing and talking softly. She eased back, scratching, and rubbing as she did until she was able to walk out of the stall.

"Damn, woman. You're definitely your father's daughter," Addie said.

"That may be the best compliment I've ever heard."

"Well hell, I thought that was when I admired your ass."

"Okay then, that was *one* of the best compliments I've ever heard."

As the women laughed, Mel looked toward the county road, seeing a one-ton pickup raising the dust and driving through the headquarters' entrance. The rails, ladders, and boxes attached to the truck made it obvious it was used for construction, even without the "Harold Jones Contractor" signs on the doors.

"Who's that?" Mel asked.

"The builders aren't quite through with the interior of the workshop. That guy drives like a bat out of hell. I've told him to slow down. Believe it or not, he did a little."

The truck came ripping through the yard, heading for one of the new metal buildings. He took a turn so fast the rear dually wheels slid, and he clipped a haystack near the building. Bales rolled and fell in haphazard order.

"Damn idiot. He'll be paying for 'em if he broke any of those bales open," Addie said. She turned to face Mel, and saw the confident horse whisperer was no longer smiling, proud of her haltering accomplishments. Mel was pale and shaking.

"Mel, you okay?"

The only answer was Mel bolting across the pen, almost vaulting over the fence, actually falling when her metal foot slipped off a rail on the far side. She was up in an instant and running awkwardly, hampered by the use of her "walking" instead of "running" foot and ankle. She disappeared behind the old barn, the one still carefully maintained and used by the Romero family for well over a century.

Addie stood, obviously shocked. She followed at a slower pace.

❧❧❧❧

For half a second, Mel saw falling hay bales then she was gone, not seeing what was before her, but what was behind, a vision that could never be forgotten. She saw the disorderly falling of earthen bricks from a destroyed wall. She heard through ears plugged by not only the sound of an explosion but also the pressure of air pushed away at a speed she couldn't even imagine. She felt the pain of a severed foot and ankle. The most horrific moment of her life was suddenly real and present, an invader in the safety of a place and among a people where she need not feel this level of pain and terror.

Mel ran; that's all she knew to do was run, find a place where she knew she was safe. In that moment, she went back nearly thirty years to a special place, a place that had been one of her greatest havens, the hiding place she and her teenaged lover had shared, hidden from invasive eyes. Mel ran. She ran to the back of the old barn.

꩜ ꩜ ꩜ ꩜

Addie found Mel behind the barn. The old bench was still there, plus two rickety metal lawn chairs, circa 1950. It was the same ones they'd nabbed from the forgotten items in the barn loft, abandoned by different generations of Romeros. Mel wasn't sitting anywhere. She paced back and forth, occasionally stopping to breathe deeply, her eyes closed. Her face was more gray than pink and there was sweat on her forehead.

"I'm here," Addie said.

Mel looked at her with haunted eyes. "I'm sorry."

"Why?"

"We were having such a good day, the best day I'd had in a long time."

Addie said nothing. She simply waited. Mel began to shiver, and tears streamed down her face. Addie came to her slowly, as though she was approaching a skittish colt. When she was close enough, she opened her arms, but didn't cross the inches still between them. Mel's face relaxed just a fraction, and she crossed those inches, accepting the comfort her first love now offered. She laid her head on Addie's shoulder and sobbed. When she spoke, her words were so muffled that Addie strained to hear and understand.

"It was the hay," Mel said. "That day, that awful day, in the moments after the explosion, earthen bricks fell from a destroyed wall, and in my confusion and pain, all I could think about was how they reminded me of the falling of poorly stacked hay."

"Cry all you want, love," Addie said. "Tell me what you want to say or be silent. Whatever you need."

It was then that Mel realized Addie shivered as

well. She stepped back, looking into Addie's eyes.

"I'm all right. Please don't let it upset you, Darlin'. I'm so sorry I spoiled our day."

"You didn't." Addie pushed loose hair from Mel's face. She reached into her back pocket and handed Mel the bandana she had stashed there. Mel laughed, then without shame, blew her nose loudly and wiped at her eyes. "Yeah, I'm worried about you, and wish I could help, but that's not why I'm shaking."

"Why, Hon? Why?"

Addie looked around this hiding place that had once been their haven.

"It was here, Mel."

"What was here?"

"This...this is where Mama caught us kissing." Tears appeared in her eyes. "This is where it all went wrong."

It was Mel's turn to open her arms. They leaned on each other, creating a unit far stronger together than they each were separately. Sometimes pain is a great catalyst for good.

Chapter Sixteen

A Surprise on the Porch

Mel looked intently at the computer screen, watching the image, occasionally wavy from poor pixelation, of her counselor, Will Gold. He leaned so far back in his office chair that Mel was concerned he might fall.

"I'll tell you again, Captain, a sleep prescription wouldn't hurt," Will said. "These nightmares must be bringing you down."

"I'd consider it if I didn't have the spring."

"Spring?" Will responded. "What's this, a new sleep technique I'd never heard about?"

Mel laughed. "No, there's a spring and cottonwood grove a few miles from the house. It's been a sacred place for me since I was a kid. I don't know why, but I sleep like the dead when I'm there. Been camping there two or three nights a week and napping during the afternoon on some days. Dreading winter when it will be too cold to sleep at the spring."

Will leaned forward, secretly relieving Mel's anxiety about his impending fall. He placed an elbow on the desk and rested his jaw in his hand. "Sounds like you've found much of what you need to heal right there in the middle of nowhere."

"City boy. You just don't understand life on the land."

"Nope, I don't. Do you have an IHOP nearby?"

Mel chuckled. "Ordering food here means trying to yell bacon out of the pan onto the plate."

"Not the life for me. Couldn't live without Saturday morning Rooty-Tooty Fresh and Fruity. Does it work on the bacon?"

"Wouldn't know. Haven't tried anything that stupid…well, at least not with bacon."

Will laughed. "You're doing better, Captain. Good to hear you make a joke."

"It's a family expectation. Being around my brother, Hoyt, has helped remind me of that."

"You're looking better, physically. Had the team conference with your primary care provider and—"

"Yes," Mel said, interrupting. "I've put on the four pounds, and I'll be bringing that half a carrot cake."

"Do I get any?"

"If I bring more, there won't be any for Hoyt and me." She reconsidered as she heard her counselor sigh deeply. "Oh, all right. I'll bring you a slice."

"Captain, are these teleconferencing sessions enough?"

"Well, I think so. Besides, there's so much happening here. Getting back in touch with the land, Addie coming home, finding a place where I can sleep, really sleep. I think I'm better here for now."

"I think you're right, but there's a new treatment for PTSD that's proving effective. It's called Comprehensive Resource Model or CRM. Works miracles with some people, but I'd need to see you regularly for a while and in person."

"What's it do?"

The therapist leaned back again, renewing Mel's

concern about his pending fall. "It's an interesting combination of techniques that help revive and then heal not only the mental memories that can be expressed by talking, but also digs into the emotions caught somewhere in the body, proving an opportunity for release. It also uses shamanic visualizations, drawing on power animals to guide them to answers through meditation. There are other components too. You might want to read up on it."

"Sounds like an awesome method." Mel paused to think. "For now, I think I'm kind of doing a lot of that by accident."

"What do you mean?"

"Well, being around horses gets me out of my head and allows me to feel without thinking about it."

"Yes, equine-assisted therapy has long been a proven benefit for PTSD."

A knock on the door caused Mel to look away from the computer screen. She was surprised because she hadn't heard a vehicle pull into the yard. *I really must have been focused on therapy*, Mel thought.

"Will, there's someone at the door."

The counselor looked toward a wall. Mel remembered the clock in his office.

"We only have a few minutes left, and this seems like a good stopping spot. See you next week? Same time on Skype?"

"That works. Bye for now, Will."

"See you in a week, Captain."

Mel closed Skype and then stood to answer the door. She opened that door just in time to see the tail end of Addie's truck scooting out of the driveway and onto the road, heading toward the Romero headquarters. *What the heck?* Mel thought, then she noticed the box resting on the porch. There was no address nor any of the labels identifying it as a UPS delivery. Duct tape held the top closed and bold marking with a wide permanent marker said, "For Mel."

"Sneaky," Mel said as she laughed at Addie's surprise techniques. She picked up the box, carrying it inside to the kitchen table. She used her pocket-knife to cut the tape, surprised at her sense of excitement at seeing what rested inside. At the very top, a layer of tissue paper beneath, was a massive package of the teriyaki beef jerky just like the jerky she and Addie shared when they were kids, as well as a retro carton of a pastry she thought no longer existed—banana cream filled pastries. Mel laughed aloud at that one. *Looks like Addie's joined the conspiracy to make me gain weight*, she thought. She lifted the two packages to the side, removed the tissue paper and then gasped at what was beneath. A pair of hand-made tapaderos rested in the bottom of the box. It was a unique design, keeping some of the shape and beauty of the huge and ornamental variety most often seen in use by the heroes of B-grade Westerns of the '50s and '60s. They were much smaller and well made, the leather matching perfectly the rough side out of her saddle. Mel looked at the underside of the leather and found the maker's mark. She felt a knot of sentimentality in her throat as she realized it was the son of the man who made her saddle. The stirrups inside were modified as well. A wedge-shaped hunk of rubber was placed on the left stirrup with the wedge lower at the front and higher at the back. Mel smiled as she wondered if the ingenious design would enable her to mount from the left. She'd try it soon. She looked out the window at the approaching dusk and decided it was too late that day.

Mel glanced at the clock, estimating how long it had been since Addie left, and realized she wouldn't have had time to get back to the Romero ranch. Taking advantage of the last of the daylight, Mel left the box on the table and walked outside, heading toward the corrals. She needed to feed Old Blue and the cow with the prolapsed uterus who was awaiting her trip to the local cattle auction. Mel felt for the old girl, knowing her pending fate, but ranching required hard choices, and that cow would never produce another calf. A bitter smile crossed her face as she realized the Navy had faced a similar choice with her.

"At least I didn't end up dog food," she whispered to herself.

It didn't take long to give Blue his evening ration of grain and hay and scatter a goodly amount of pure alfalfa (livestock ambrosia) in the feeder for the cow. Mel was doing her best to make the old girl's last days as pleasant as possible. When she got back to the house, she used the house phone to call the Romero home, still remembering a phone number she hadn't dialed for thirty years. Even if she hadn't remembered, it didn't matter. A paper posted beside the phone had the number, faded and written in her mother's neat script.

"Romero Ranch," Addie's voice responded after the third ring.

"Seems like the good fairy came to my house," Mel said.

"Hmm…who might that be?"

"Oh, I suspect it was some crazy lady who just moved home from California."

"My oh my, a crazy lady, you said?"

"Yep. Crazy as a loon, but in a good way," Mel responded.

"Why you say that?"

"Crazy enough to read the minds of horses and to know what an old, injured sailor truly needs."

"Yeah, I'd say that's a good crazy."

"Why'd you leave?"

"I like leaving surprises."

Mel chuckled. "I hit the jackpot on this one." There was a pause. Mel didn't have to see Addie to envision the woman's pleased smile.

"Think they'll work?"

"The tapaderos or the banana creams?"

"Both, and the jerky."

"Jerky is a guaranteed 'yes.' Tapaderos and Banana Flips are yet to be tested. The first will have to wait until tomorrow. Why don't you come back and help me test out the latter?"

"Tonight?"

"Heck yeah. Why not? Did I tell you Hoyt had the place hooked up with satellite TV and internet? There's a show I want you to see."

"Yeah, is it on tonight?"

"Oh, come on. You can't be behind the times. Haven't had to wait for a show's scheduled time for years. It's on HBO."

"Okay then. Had dinner?"

"Nope, but I have a pot of Texas chili in the refrigerator that I made yesterday. Plenty for both of us."

"Papa made tortillas today. I'll bring some of those."

Mel chuckled again. "Amazes me that your dad

was secretly a really good cook."

"Mama had a desperate need to be the best, so he just let her have that title."

"Get your ass over here. I'm hungry. I'll put the chili on the stove. Banana pastries for dessert."

Mel did as promised, taking the pot of chili from the refrigerator and putting it on low on the stove. She then walked to the master bathroom beside her bedroom where she brushed her hair and teeth, wishing she had time for a shower. In the bedroom, she paused to remove the ancient denim shirt she was wearing, replacing it with a shirt she hadn't worn since before her latest deployment to Iraq. True, it didn't hang quite as well on her still too-thin form, but it looked nice. Mel looked in the mirror and laughed. *Guess I'm getting ready for a date,* she thought.

It would appear that Addie had a similar dilemma, considering she arrived a full half-hour later than Mel had expected. Mel noticed that Addie too wore "go to town" clothing, and there was a distinct sight of fresh mascara, not to mention the subtle odor of perfume as Addie entered the house, a plastic bag of fresh tortillas in one hand and a bottle of merlot in the other.

"Wine," Mel said. "Guess I should have made special chili."

"A meal with you is darned special as far as I'm concerned," Addie responded.

Mel looked at her childhood friend, surprised at Addie's directness. "Truth be known, I feel the same."

They chatted like the old friends they were as Mel set the table, placing her box of new goodies on the small table resting below the wall phone in the kitchen. Addie walked to the drawer where she had formerly watched Mel's parents retrieve various cooking utensils. She smiled with pleasure as she found the corkscrew exactly where she expected.

"What's this show we're watching?" Addie asked as they dug into the chili, dipping bits of tortilla into the hearty mixture of meat, tomato sauce, beans, and red chili powder. Mel sipped the wine approvingly, realizing it was an ideal choice for the Texas chili.

"It's called Gentleman Jack and based on the true story of an early nineteenth Century English lesbian. She's quite a character."

"More so than you?"

"Puts me to shame," Mel responded.

When the meal was done and the dishes in the sink, they both refilled their wine glasses and moved to the living room. The ancient console TV that Mel's parents had used for many years was gone, now stored in a back corner of the old barn. The flat screen TV Mel bought had a screen four times the size of the old TV screen and included a bank of four speakers. They both took seats on the couch across from the TV. Mel turned on the satellite receiver and the TV using the remote but left it on the soundless home screen for HBO.

"Kick your boots off and put your feet up if you want," Mel said as she kicked off her right boot, placing her one foot on the coffee table.

"Sounds good," Addie answered as she placed her wine glass on the table then did as instructed, stretching her legs before her and placing stocking feet on the table. She looked pointedly at Mel's left leg. "Wouldn't you be more comfortable if you could put both legs up?"

"Well, yeah, but I have to drop my pants to take

off the prosthesis."

Addie looked at Mel with a subtle smile and a twinkle in her eye. "That would be a bad thing because...?"

Mel laughed, then stood, unceremoniously undoing buckle and button then unzipping her pants. They dropped to just below her knees, and she quickly undid the contraption above her knee that held the artificial foot and ankle in place. Pulling up her pants, she then sat back on the couch and pulled the artificial foot free, sighing in pleasure as she did so. She stretched her legs, putting her foot on the table and the left leg still almost entirely on the couch.

"I take it that felt good. Is it like taking off your shoes?" Addie asked.

"More like taking off a bra."

"I hear you there," Addie said, looking thoughtful, as though deciding something. "Speaking of which." Addie reached behind herself with both hands, made a quick unhooking motion, pulled both bra straps below her sleeves to release them and then pulled the entire contraption out from just above the "V" at the neck of her blouse. She then sighed in relief.

"That was fun to watch," Mel said.

"More fun to do. Lean forward."

Mel blushed. "Uh, I'm wearing a sports bra." She picked up Addie's bra, which now rested on the couch between them. It was black with red lace. "Lace?" Mel asked, a note of surprise in her voice.

"What of it? I like pretty underwear. Makes me feel special."

"Well, you didn't feel that way when we were teenagers."

"When I was a teenager, Mom bought my underwear, and she was a white cotton woman to the core."

Mel looked at the tag on the bra. "Victoria Secret?" she said in surprise.

"Well, okay. That one was a gift."

"The movie star?"

"Yeah." Addie blushed. "One of my more glorious and entertaining mistakes."

"At least it helped me keep up with you through the entertainment news."

Addie sighed. "I hope this isn't the first of many future reminders to come."

Mel reached up to briefly stroke Addie's cheek. "Teasing is a sign of affection."

"I know." Addie looked to where the end of Mel's jean leg hung flaccid past the end of her stump. "Do you mind if I see it?"

"Not at all," Mel answered. "I consider it one of the miracles of modern medicine."

Mel pulled up her pants' leg and exposed the end of her abbreviated leg. Addie leaned close, looking at the surprisingly smooth skin. She reached down and gently stroked the stump. Mel made a sharp intake of breath, and Addie pulled her hand away.

"Did I hurt you?" Addie asked.

"No. It's just that"—Mel took a deep breath—"the only ones to touch it have been doctors, nurses, and technicians. It's the first time someone has touched it...lovingly."

Addie's mischievous smile returned along with the twinkle in her eye. "You mean like this?" She returned to gently stroking the stump and then let her hand drift up the inner part of Mel's leg, past the knee and as far as she could reach before the jean's leg let her go no farther.

"Yeah, like that." Mel leaned forward, initiating a kiss that deepened and became heated almost immediately, each set of arms pulling the other woman closer. After a time, Mel paused and pulled slightly away. "If we keep this up, we won't see the show."

Addie laughed breathily. "As someone recently pointed out to me, it's the age of the Internet. We can watch any time we want."

Mel's hand moved to cup a bra-free breast with her right hand. It was Addie's turn for a sharp intake of breath.

"Will your father worry if you spend the night?"

Addie responded with a chuckle. "The last thing he said before I left was, 'I won't wait up.' He had that sly grin he gets sometimes."

"Can I lean on you to the bedroom?" Mel said.

"I thought you'd never ask."

Mel turned off the TV and satellite receiver. It might have been easier just to hop to the bedroom, like she did many nights, but she truly enjoyed leaning on and being held close by the lover whom she'd never forgotten and with whom she now had hope of a rich future.

Chapter Seventeen

Tapaderos

Mel awoke and stretched across the bed, reaching for a woman who was no longer there. She wondered at Addie's absence, at the same time realizing that she had actually slept an entire night. *Sex is a great sleep aid,* she thought. Mel sat up, rubbing her eyes sleepily, looking about the room and toward the adjoining bathroom. The door was open with no sight nor sound indicating Addie was within.

"Where'd you go?" Mel said to the empty room. She hopped to the bathroom for an abbreviated morning ritual before returning to the bedroom where she quickly donned her prosthesis and clothes. She fought a mild fear that Addie regretted their night together now that it was the light of day. For herself, Mel had no doubts whatsoever. She felt like her heart had come home, and her body was pretty darned happy about new developments as well.

She went down the hallway to the kitchen, catching a whiff of coffee along the way. The coffee carafe was nearly full, one used cup in the sink and a half-eaten banana pastry on a plate on the counter. The sight of that simple piece of trash food brought a smile to Mel's face. She and Addie had shared a passion for those tidbits as their favorite after-school snack. Mel picked up the pastry and took a bite. She chewed twice and then stared in surprise at the delicacy in her hand. "Damn, that's sweet," she said. If she'd doubted it before, Mel truly knew she now had the taste buds of an adult. Considering the half-eaten morsel on the plate, she suspected Addie had the same reaction. *Maybe Mellie will like them.* Mel considered giving the whole box to her niece.

As though decades hadn't passed, Mel looked automatically to the aging chalk board hanging by the service porch door, the place where family had always left messages. "In the tack-room," was written in handwriting Mel could still recognize as Addie's. Mel pulled two thermal cups from the cabinet, dolloped milk and sugar in both before topping them off from the coffee pot. A cup in each hand, she left the house, walking directly across the farmyard to the box-car tack-room. The doors were wide open, and Mel wondered what had motivated her first love and her new lover to abandon a warm bed for the morning chill. Mel managed the high step into the boxcar, despite her absent foot, without spilling a drop of coffee.

"What the heck are you doing?" she asked as she waited for her eyes to adjust to the darker interior.

"Saving your life, that's what I'm doing," Addie responded.

As her eyes adjusted, Mel realized it was her saddle upon which Addie focused her full attention. A screwdriver and pliers rested on the seat of Hoyt's sad-dle, the one adjacent to Mel's on the saddle-rack. Be-side the tools rested the stirrups originally placed on Mel's saddle by a long-ago saddle-maker. Mel blinked back tears as she realized Addie's task. She was plac-ing the last of the new tapaderos on Mel's saddle. The other was already in place.

"I been worried sick you were going to get that metal contraption you walk on stuck in a stirrup."

"Must admit I was a tad worried myself." Mel found herself blinking back tears, deeply touched by Addie's caring.

"At least you got some sense," Addie said. She finished tightening the bolt that held the stirrup in the leathers, then she gave the stirrup a good yank to make sure it was solid. "That'll do."

"Addie."

"What?"

"Thank you."

Addie smiled and moved to Mel, putting her arms around the woman, leaning in for a kiss. It was gentle and sweet, and Mel thought it was just fine.

"I'd hug you back, but I'd spill coffee down your back," Mel whispered against her lover's cheek.

"Bless you. You brought coffee." Addie took a step back, taking one cup from Mel's hand. "That one cup I had wasn't enough. Oh, and uh...I hope you're not disappointed but..."

"The banana pastry tastes like over sweet wallpaper paste."

"Yep."

"It's hard to think how much we loved those things."

"I think your mother kept them for us because she knew none of the adults would steal them from the kids," Addie said.

"Then I suppose you won't mind if I give them to Mellie."

"Oh gawd, please do. They're nasty."

Mel sipped at her coffee as she moved to admire

the new addition to her saddle. "How did Andy match the leather so close?"

"He had some old rough-side-out leather his dad used. May have been from the same leather he used to make your saddle. It's not quite as aged as your saddle—having been stored out of the sun all these years—but it's close."

Mel raised the tapadero and touched the leather, a caress actually.

"Addie."

"Yes 'um?"

"I love you too."

Addie stepped behind Mel, wrapping her non-coffee-holding arm over Mel's shoulder and across her chest. "I never got over you, you know."

"Maybe there's something to this twin flame thing. I never felt about any woman the way I felt... still feel about you."

Mel took Addie's hand as she turned around and led her to the open doorway. The sun was fully up now, and there was warmth in the light. They sat on the doorsill, drinking their coffee in comfortable silence.

"We'll put those tapaderos to the test today," Mel said, breaking the silence.

"How's that?"

"Hoyt and Sammy are coming out this morning, and we're going to gather the south pasture and move the cattle down to the corner pasture adjacent to the Dodson place."

"Think Tom would mind if I rode his bay gelding?"

Mel chuckled. "Not a bit. If we put a greenhorn on, he'd be upset, but he'd be pleased to know the famous three-time World Champion Cowgirl Addie Romero was exercising his horse while he's away at college."

Addie blushed, and Mel enjoyed the sight of Addie's pleasure and discomfort.

"Shut up you," Addie said. "That was a long time ago. Want to know a secret?"

"What?"

"Half the time I was getting all those belt buckles and prize money, I kept wondering if you could beat me."

"Guess what."

"What?"

"I couldn't. I was good, but never as good as you." Mel stood, grasping Addie's hand and pulling her to her feet. "Come on. We need some real breakfast before Hoyt puts us to work."

They'd finished their bacon and eggs and were drinking yet another cup of coffee when Hoyt's pickup pulled into the drive. Mel laughed aloud as she saw her brother walk toward Addie's pickup, a shit-eating grin on his face.

"Guess he figured things out," Addie said.

"I'm looking forward to the teasing."

Sammy scrapped his boots on the mat beside the back door then gave a perfunctory knock at the door before entering. His father wasn't far behind.

"Got any more coffee?" Sammy asked. He took off his hat, holding it in his hand as he looked at Addie. "Hello, ma'am," the young man said.

"That's right. You two haven't met, have you?" Mel asked.

"Sammy, son. This here is Addie Romero," Hoyt said.

Sammy's eyes widened. "You're the one who owns Flag 'Em Down, the Kentucky Derby winner."

Mel laughed. "That amongst other things."

"Morning, Addie. Long time no see," Hoyt said.

"Always a pleasure, Hoyt. You're still my big brother whether you want to be or not."

Hoyt's grin got even bigger, and his eyes twinkled. "So, are you here awful early, or did you stay really late?"

"What do you think?" Addie responded, blushing as she grinned.

Sammy looked back and forth between the three adults, grasping the situation. "Uh, Aunt Mel."

"What, Sammy?"

"Does this mean I have two aunts?"

Mel reached across the table to hold Addie's hand. "It sure does, dear nephew. It sure does."

Chapter Eighteen

Demons and Dreams

The sprite and the naiad sat comfortably together on a high tree branch. They looked down at the women sleeping near the base of the sprite's tree home, the oldest of the old cottonwoods surrounding the ancient spring. Silence and time bothered neither of the immortals. For them, the hours of sleeping for the humans they watched were only flashing instants. The two spirits sat close with their arms intertwined. Over the centuries, they had grown to love each other as much as the water and trees they tended.

Darkness gathered in a cloud around the one woman sleeping below, sleeping in the arms of her lover. The sprite raised her hand, ready to wave away the darkness as she had so many times before. Gently, the naiad placed her hand over her companion's, stopping the motion.

"She is ready," the naiad said, the tinkling sound of water to her voice. "And she is no longer alone."

The sprite lowered her hand and nodded in silent agreement. They watched.

❧❧❧❧

Mel looked into the eyes of a woman who should

be dead, but those eyes still shone with a spark of life. As she pulled the small boy toward her, Mel looked into those eyes and said a promise that she meant with all her heart.

"I'll take care of him," she said.

The words were barely voiced when the spark of life left the eyes of the dying mother. Mel was astounded at the woman's strength and determination to hold to life, to protect her child, despite injuries that should have killed her instantly. As Mel rolled onto her back, she pulled the boy onto her chest, gently turning his head so that he could not see the sight of devastated flesh that had been his parents. As she pulled his head to her chest, stroking his hair and offering comforting, shushing noises to the child, he cried with a passion that had to have been heard in heaven itself. So intense was her focus on the plight of the boy she barely felt the agony of her severed foot and ankle. Awkwardly, she crawled, half rolled onto her left side, pulling herself forward and using her body to shield the child from the sight of his devastated parents and holding him close with her right hand and arm. She made her way toward a bit of shade from a still standing wall. With the roof of the café decimated, the heat of the sunshine only added to the agonies.

Another miracle came as her hand fell on a bit of flimsy plastic that she felt through the dust, and her fingers wrapped around a cheap water bottle. The object had only a small hole near the top, contrary to the devastation that surrounded it. She held it as she finished covering the small distance to the desperately needed shade. Once there, she collapsed onto her back, and the boy now clung to her so that she felt as well as heard his hiccupy sobs. She opened the bottle and offered it to the boy, who sat up and drank deeply as she held it to his mouth. When he was done, Mel drank as well, knowing she needed the fluid to help compensate for blood loss. She put the cap back on the bottle and set it within easy reach, comforted by the sight of the water still inside. As she laid back, the boy rested atop of her, clinging to her desperately. Mel wrapped her arms around the child, striving to remember what comforted her when she was a child. As she sought memories, her mind recalled her mother's voice.

"Way down yonder, in the meadow, all the pretty little horses," she sang, just as her mother had sung to her. The boy's sobs lessened. "When you wake you shall find, all the pretty little horses. Dapples and grays, pintos and bays, all the pretty little horses." The boy's sobs stopped, and she felt him relax atop her. "Way down yonder, in the meadow, all the pretty little horses."

As her voice faded, she realized the child was asleep. With that, her mind could take no more, and she slipped into unconsciousness.

꙳ ꙳ ꙳ ꙳

Mel awoke, her face already covered in tears, and she voiced an involuntary groan from a pain so intense it had to be heard. Addie was immediately awake. She sat up and threw back the sleeping bag that covered them both.

"What? What is it?" Addie demanded.

"I remember," Mel said, taking a shaky breath. "I know what I did."

Addie lay back down and wrapped not only her arms but her whole body around her shivering lover.

"What, Love. What do you remember?"

"I promised."

"Promised what?"

"To take care of him."

"Who?"

"The boy."

"The boy from the explosion? The one who was crying?"

"Yes." Mel took deep breaths, striving to control the caldron of emotions. She needed to share what she now remembered with the woman who mattered more to her than anyone else in the world. Anyone, except possibly a boy, one she had no name for and not a clue how to find.

"His mother kept herself alive. I don't know how that devastated body could still be alive. What strength there is in motherhood." Mel looked not into the distance but into the past as she continued. "She didn't let herself die until I promised. She gave me her son to care for, to be safe."

"You did, Darling. You did."

"For a time, for a few moments." Mel turned to face Addie, wrapping her arms around her, adding her strength to the embrace. "I lost consciousness. When I finally awoke, my aide, Lieutenant Canton, was beside me, and they were loading me into a military ambulance. I asked him where the boy was, and he was confused. He just wanted to know what boy."

"Oh Darling, how awful."

"While I was in the field hospital, I asked around as best I could, but you can't do much from a cot in a field hospital with no communications. No one could help."

Addie pulled back slightly. In the full moonlight, she was able to look clearly into her lover's eyes.

"I don't know why"—Addie said—"but I've been given this ungodly talent to make money. If money can buy what it takes to find him, I promise you, we will."

"Canton looked without any luck. I'll ask Sherine, Zadab's cousin, if she can help."

"Sherine?"

"She runs a network of women's shelters in Iraq."

"We'll find him. In my heart of hearts, I believe we'll find him," Addie said.

Mel's shivering lessened. Amazingly, she was fully asleep in an instant. Addie gently moved a lock of hair from where it was plastered against Mel's cheek, held there by still drying tears. Pulling the sleeping bag back over them both, Addie lay beside Mel, studying every feature of her lover's face.

"What a woman you are," she whispered. "We will find him. Goddess willing, we'll find him."

There was a musical feel to the air around them. There was the tinkle of water and rustle of leaves. For a moment, Addie thought maybe she heard voices in the breeze.

⁂

At daybreak, she and Mel rode different directions, both going to their separate homes to begin their quest to find the boy.

Addie spent most of the morning on the telephone or the computer. She'd even called her way-too-famous ex, soliciting help. Fortunately, Hollywood connections meant a number of avenues and people who knew their way around the private investigation world. Her morning's work netted a list of seven private investigators, and her search of websites narrowed that down to three. Already, she had video conferences scheduled with two and left messages for the third.

Maybe we need to come up with a name for this young fella, Addie thought. *Doesn't seem right to just call him "the boy."* She stood on the porch outside the kitchen door, contemplating the dilemma and drinking her fifth cup of coffee. She started slightly when the door opened abruptly, and her father stood in the open doorway.

"Any luck finding someone to look for Melinda's *hijo*?" he asked.

Addie looked at her father, surprised. *Ask and ye shall receive*, she thought. *Hijo...my son. That's a good name for now.*

"Good timing, Papa. I was just thinking we needed something better to call this mystery kid other than 'the boy.'"

"*Hijo*? A good name. Will Melinda like it?"

They both looked down the county road running by their front gate. In the distance, Mel's new Explorer was raising the dust and headed their direction.

"Looks like we'll find out soon enough." She glanced at her father. "To answer your question, I have contacts for three highly recommended private investigators, all of whom have worked in the Middle East."

"Good." Alfredo slapped the newspaper that he held against his thigh.. "You greet Melinda. I haven't read my papers yet."

They both entered the kitchen with Alfredo taking a seat at the table where *The Wallstreet Journal* and the *Dallan Weekly News* awaited his attention. The old man would be at the computer later, catching up on news too recent to have made print. Still, Addie knew he would never give up his love of the smell of newsprint and ink. Addie started to refill her cup when she decided six cups of coffee had to be one too many. Instead, she reached in the cabinet for a clean cup, adding milk and sugar before filling it with coffee. Then she exited the kitchen and waited, cup in hand, by the driveway as Mel's Explorer came to a stop beside her. Mel stepped out of the vehicle and Addie handed her the coffee.

"Curb service?" Mel asked as she took the coffee.

Addie laughed. "The only curb we have around here are one or two curb bits out in the tack room."

Mel smiled and reached to stroke Addie's cheek. She closed the driver's door to her SUV and leaned against the vehicle as she took a drink of coffee.

"Perfect," Mel said.

"Me or the coffee?"

"Yes."

Addie laughed. "I like the way you think."

"It took some doing, but I finally got hold of Sherine, and we talked via video conference," Mel said. "She's got awesome connections throughout Iraq. I'm hoping that pays off. I managed to reach Admiral Wells, too. He'll do all he can to expedite anything we need there in Iraq. Couldn't reach Canton so I sent him an email. The Admiral said he'd give him release time to visit Baghdad to see what he can find."

"Canton?"

"Lieutenant Harry Canton. He was my aide when I was with Navy CentCom—the one who found me and drug me out of the rubble. The boy was already gone when he found me."

"And I tracked down three likely candidates for an investigator."

Mel looked at Addie intently, eyeing her lover over the rim of her coffee cup. "You don't have to do this, you know. An investigator will cost a small fortune. This is my problem, not yours."

"The hell it isn't. If it affects you, it affects me." Addie opened the kitchen door and walked inside, Mel following closely behind.

The crease between her eyes deepened as Mel thought how to respond. "I'd feel the same way, but it's hard for me to ask you to get involved in something that may be hopeless."

"Hopeless? What is it your daddy used to say?"

"You're a Morris, and Morrises don't give up." Mel chuckled then downed the last of her coffee. "So, what do we do next?"

Addie took the empty cup and led Mel back to the kitchen. "First, we put this cup in the sink, so Papa won't nag at me for losing it. Then we work with horses. There's a filly I want you to start training for reining. Just because I moved home from California doesn't mean my business can afford for me to neglect the show circuit."

"I didn't bring my saddle."

"Don't worry about that."

"I thought you were the one having nightmares about me getting my metal foot caught in the stirrup."

"I did."

"So? I told you, I forgot my saddle."

"*Hola,* Melinda," Alfredo said, a well-timed interruption to the conversation. He lowered the *Journal* just enough to make eye-contact with Mel.

"Morning, Alfredo. What's in today's news?"

"Insanity and stupidity," he responded. "Another normal day."

Addie ran a little water in the cup, gave it a quick wash, and put it in the drain rack with the rest of the morning dishes. "Papa, we'll be around if you need me. Going to do some training out in the arena."

"Is that what you call it—the arena? You could add bleachers and have rodeos with what you had built."

Addie glanced toward Mel. "You know, that's not a bad idea."

"You could add roping chutes, and we could at least do team ropings. Good money makers, I've heard."

A faraway look kidnapped Addie's expression. "Maybe an RV Park."

"Oh dear, see what you've done, Alfredo. Now she's planning another venture."

"My hija. She does well with her ventures."

"*Hija*...that reminds me, Mel. Papa and I decided the boy needs a name."

"Good idea."

"How do you feel about us calling him *Hito,* short for Mel's *Hijo?*"

Mel's face took on a soft smile. "I like it a lot."

Addie laughed. "That's one decision made. Follow me, Captain Morris. We have work to do."

"Captain Morris?" Mel echoed. "Captain or not, I have this sudden realization that you may outrank me."

Addie opened the door and Mel exited first before Addie stepped outside, closing the door behind herself. "In this place I do." She tapped Mel definitively on the shoulder. "This is my operation."

"Wouldn't even think about arguing that point."

As they walked across the yard toward the barn, Addie pointed out the bay filly she wanted Mel to train. She explained horsey details, including how many saddlings the filly was into her training and background on any lessons learned about the personality of that one, particular horse. The young horse was green, early in her "schooling." Addie knew it was a challenge Mel would love.

"So, what are we going to do about a saddle addressing my handicap?"

"All taken care of."

Addie flipped a switch, illuminating the tack room, and she led Mel to a saddle already sporting her specially designed tapaderos. At the sight of the saddle, Mel inhaled sharply, obviously stunned.

It wasn't the simple rough-side-out or smooth leather of a working saddle. The leather was meticulously tooled, even the tapaderos, and there were tastefully placed tidbits of silver on the skirts and around the edge of the horn. It was a show saddle, a saddle worthy of being a trophy at any of the major rodeos. On the fenders, where a trophy saddle would sport the name of the rodeo and the prize, a message was tooled into the leather with a decorative circle around it.

"CAPT Melinda Morris-Veteran-USN" was embossed in the leather and dyed a slightly darker shade of brown.

Mel stood, mouth open, obviously shocked. "Addie, that must have—"

"Don't you dare say anything about how much it cost." Addie shuffled nervously. "Do you like it?"

"Like?" Mel asked. "Like, you ask?" She stood silent, shaking her head, and searching for words. "In all my days, I have never felt so loved and honored."

Mel grabbed Addie by the front of her shirt and pulled her lover to her. Is there a description for a kiss like that, a kiss that said more than words ever could? It was more like two powerful souls joining together, sending sparks into the universe.

Chapter Nineteen

Honor the Flag

*O*ut in ranch country, the term "neighbor" was defined in a way that few city folk could comprehend. No one else lived in the same "block" of the ranch headquarters and line camps scattered over at least a hundred square miles. Yet people there shared a closeness rarely found where paved streets and neat sidewalks ruled the world. When it was time to wean, brand, or to ship cattle to market, the basic concept of "neighboring" made everyone able to complete tasks none of them could accomplish alone. From one place to the next, folks worked together as teams, gathering cattle, systematically dehorning, branding, and, when appropriate, castrating. Herds were gathered to various pens when they were sorted according to destination or purpose. Even more importantly, if fire, tornado, blizzard, or illness came to this massive neighborhood, there was no such thing as an enemy. Everyone helped whoever needed the aid *du jour*. That's how they survived.

It's not just work and disaster that brings these distant neighbors together. Sometimes life needs celebration. Dancing boots, pristine and clean Stetsons, and fancy, frilly dresses needed to come out of the closet sometimes. Weddings, christenings, special birthdays, and anniversaries...there was a plethora of excuses to call together neighbors and have one helluva party.

Alfredo Romero felt that having both girls back home again merited a party, and the excuse was Fourth of July. No invitations were sent out. Word spread through the rural post office, Friday afternoon at the cattle auction in Dallan, various Sunday services, or, if some cherished neighbor wasn't available at any of those, there was always the telephone or the internet. Word got out. That's what mattered.

The old barbeque pit hadn't been used in years. Hoyt, Sammy, and Mellie joined Alfredo, Addie, and Mel in the task of digging out the old pit, collecting wood, and preparing two huge chunks of brisket and one of *cabrito* (tender, young goat) for that specialty feast known as real pit barbeque. The meat was rolled in a mixture of salt and brown sugar, wrapped in butcher paper then burlap and tied with string. Now packaged, the meat was thrown into a water filled #10 washtub until it was time to be placed on the coals. When the coals were ready, packages of meat were thrown inside, and the pit was sealed at the top with a metal cover and then buried. Addie and Mel camped outside the night the wood had to be lit. For the coals to be perfect for cooking, a middle-of-the-night ignition was required. Treated with a mixture of diesel and gasoline, that wood was ready to burn. When their alarm went off at three a.m., the two women crawled out of sleeping bags and lit the old-fashioned torch they prepared the day before. Standing some distance back, Mel threw the torch onto the wood that was stacked two feet above the top of the pit. With a "woosh," the wood was alight, a sight that caught the attention of the horses across the yard in the barn and paddock. In the dark, the woman could hear a chorus of neighs and the clip-clop of horses trotting or loping around the field. As the fire settled to a steady burn, the horses quieted, and the two women stood, arms around each other, watching the glory of the fire. One of the ranch pickups now held a 250-gallon water tank and an attached pressure sprayer. On a small trailer attached to Hoyt's ATV was a fifty-gallon version of the same operation. In addition, attached to Addie's belt was a radio loaned by the local volunteer fire company along with instructions on how to initiate a page should the fire turn cranky. All went well, and neither woman regretted the loss of sleep for this one special night.

Other dishes for the feast came in the form of pot-luck contributions as well as it being a BYOC (bring your own chair) event. Borrowed from the old schoolhouse that served as the community center were long tables that rapidly filled with all forms of salads, casseroles, and deserts with one table dedicated entirely to the main attraction—pit barbequed meat. Mel made her specialty coconut cream pie along with the now required blueberry pie, and Addie worked with her father to produce a plethora of *empañadas,* including apple, pumpkin, and peach. Susan had received so many requests for her carrot cake that she brought two. Local gardens were obviously doing well, apparent in the many versions of squash and green bean dishes adorning the tables. The new concrete apron outside Addie's main barn was converted into a dance floor, and a local band of aging musicians from Dallan had been hired for the event. The party was likely to be memorable.

Hoyt, Susan, and the kids brought from town a special guest, one checked out for the day from the

Dallan Senior Care Services. Since coming back to the ranch, Mel had taken to visiting her mother at the rest home at least once a week, usually checking the woman out of the facility for a trip to the local drive-in for ice cream. Conversations could be confusing but gratifying. As the Alzheimer's scrambled memories in her mother's mind, being around the woman was almost like living in a time machine, figuring out the confusion as to whether it was 1950 or 2001. Mel just went with the flow.

Being with Mom now, that's almost worth losing a foot, Mel thought one day as she licked at her own vanilla ice cream cone, reaching across the front seat to wipe a wayward streak of cream from her mother's chin. At that moment, as far as her mother was concerned, Mel was Aunt Cricket—a woman dead before Mel was born—and Marleen Morris was telling her aunt how much she loved playing basketball. Mel piped in now and again with a "that's good, honey" or "proud you made the high score." At this stage, Mel found Alzheimer's to have an unexpected and odd gift. She learned more about her mother's early years than she'd ever known before, and for the first time in her life, she fully comprehended that this mother she loved had once been a child, a teen, a blushing bride of nineteen.

Today was different. While the whole Morris family was busy, sub-hosts to the big party, each one also took a turn in a designated lawn chair, carefully positioned in the shade near the main house. Resting in the next chair was the queen of the day, Marleen Morris. Since coming home, this was Mel's first time to see her mother back in ranch country, at a neighbor's house that was almost an extension of the Morris Ranch headquarters. For a time, it felt like the matriarch had come home.

"You have all you need, Mama?" Mel asked, giving her mother's hand a squeeze where it rested on the arm of her lawn chair.

"Why Lordie, yes. Always did love these big shindigs, but that music sure sounds kinda funny. I prefer Bob Wills, you know."

"Yes, ma'am, I do, but we couldn't get him. It's some of the local folks."

"Or Patsy Cline. Can any of the locals sing 'Crazy'?" She leaned conspiratorially toward her daughter, lowering her voice to a whisper. "Don't tell anyone, but that song always makes me think about Ruth Romero. Bless her heart, that woman isn't playing with a full deck."

Mel laughed with a mixture of shock and humor. "Mama, you don't know the half of it."

"Poor little Addie. I fear she catches the worst of it."

The humor evaporated as Mel looked at her mother. "Mama, you still don't know the half of it."

Addie arrived, carrying two paper plates, one holding a slice of carrot cake and the other a pumpkin *empanada*. She set the carrot cake on the small TV tray positioned in front of Marleen, and she handed the second to Mel.

"I figured you two might be ready for dessert," Addie said. She kneeled in front of Mel, placing one hand on Mel's knee, and the other atop the two hands of mother and daughter. "It's so fine to see you, Mrs. Morris."

For a moment, Marleen stared at Addie with intensity. Mel watched as something changed in her mother's eyes. She'd seen that change a time or two before and knew that, for a few moments at least, her mother was fully in the present. The older woman gently extracted her hand from the two hands that covered it, and she reached to stroke Addie's cheek.

"Sweet child." The old woman's eyes glistened with unshed tears. "You didn't deserve what your mama did to you." One tear escaped and trickled down a convoluted path on a wrinkled cheek. "I'm so sorry, child. Jim and I just couldn't figure what to do to help."

At that point Marleen wasn't the only one with glistening eyes. "Dear *Tia*, you did more than you know," Addie answered.

Marleen let out a huff and pulled her hand back to her lap. As Mel watched her mother's eyes, she realized that the woman was gone again, living somewhere in an undesignated past.

"Well, Melinda, where has that father of yours gone?"

Mel glanced at Addie, noting the surprise on her lover's face. She'd warned Addie about Marleen's status, but hearing about it and seeing it were two different things.

"I imagine he's around here somewhere, Mama." Mel thought that likely the truth.

"But he's busy. Can I get something for you?"

"I'd sure like another batch of that brisket before I set into this great cake."

Mel stood, gently pulling Addie into the chair beside her mother. "I'll go get you some, Mama."

Addie slipped easily into the role of caretaker. As Mel walked away, she heard her mother telling Addie all about the quilt the women at the community center were working to finish before winter. There'd be a raffle at the next community meeting to see who got to take it home. Mel remembered that quilt. One they'd finished thirty years ago.

It was starting to turn dusk, and every yard light in the place was lit up, as were the Tiki torches placed at strategic sites, and camp lanterns on the serving tables. Mel was returning with a plate of meat and sauce, when she saw Alfredo take the microphone from the stand where the band had been playing. She put the plate on the TV tray before her mother. All conversation ceased around them as people waited to hear the words of the host. Alfredo had been county commissioner for many years, a fact which aided the man in developing an unexpected talent for public speaking. People remembered.

"Thank you all for being here," Alfredo started. "If you didn't come, my refrigerator couldn't hold all that meat, so you've done me a great favor." A ripple of laughter progressed through the crowd. "You all know we're here to celebrate the Fourth, something some of you may think odd for an old *norteño* like me, but next year the party may be on *Cinco de Mayo.*" Another ripple of laughter. "This year, the Fourth is extra special for me, in a way for all of us. You can see my daughter has come home, and brought a lot of new barns, machinery, and her beautiful horses. How else could I show it off without a party?"

"Keep the barns, I want more brisket," called a voice from the crowd, a slight hint of too much beer in the tone.

"Good. Addie wouldn't want you to take the barn home. It wouldn't fit in your truck," Alfredo quipped. More laughter. He allowed a pause for silence, quietly gathering the crowd back to him as effectively as he'd ever been at herding cattle. "I'm proud of my daughter and all she's done. I'm happy to have her home, but, as you all know, we have two who have come home, and, in many ways, it feels as though they are both daughters of my heart." There was a slight crack to his voice, and he took a deep breath before he continued. "It is the Fourth of July, a special date for our country. Could there be a better time to welcome home our warrior? One of our own who made history as one of the first women to command a US Navy ship. One who frightened us all when news came of her injury before we knew of the outcome." Alfredo himself had served his four years in the Army as a young man. He knew how to salute, a training he never forgot. "I welcome home Navy Captain Melinda Morris. The wars left you not entirely whole, but know that for us, you are all hero." He saluted.

The event was obviously planned. At that instant, a spotlight illuminated a hastily raised flagpole with the Stars and Stripes flying. The little band began a bad rendition of the Star-Spangled Banner, and one sole rocket flew high, then burst into a hundred lights above the crowd. Those not already standing did so, even Marleen Morris, with the help of Addie. Mel snapped to attention, giving her own salute, knowing she violated Navy protocol, saluting without being in uniform but, in that moment, she cared not a rat's ass about protocol. Behind her, she heard her mother speak loud enough for all nearby to hear.

"My daughter's in the Navy, you know. We're very proud of her."

Mel wept, knowing that no Navy band, nor Washington ceremony could ever make her feel as proud, honored, humbled, and loved as she did in that moment.

Chapter Twenty

An Old Dream

Folks helped with the clean-up during the final hour of a party that would become a local legend. Despite that help, the Romeros, Morrises, and Addie's hired hands worked for two days to turn the Romero headquarters back into a ranch instead of an oversized, outdoor honky-tonk. The mystery of two apparently abandoned pickup trucks was solved the next morning when all present heard Joe Bob's reaction upon entering the hay barn for morning feeding.

"What the hell you doing here?" he yelled.

Mel, Addie, and Hoyt were nearby, loading folding tables into Hoyt's pickup so he could take them back to the community center. They all turned their attention from the task at hand, looking curiously toward the barn. Their curiosity was quenched as they saw three cowboys stumble from the barn, into the sunlight, an angry Joe Bob following in their wake. All three looked a little worse for wear, bits of hay clinging to their clothes, and one had his Stetson on backwards.

"What do you think this is, a Motel 6?" Joe Bob demanded. "That hay's for feeding, not sleeping."

The three men made for their pickup as fast as they could run, Joe Bob at their heels. Despite its age, the faded blue truck started the first time, and they sprayed gravel as they made for the county road.

Hoyt chuckled at the sight. "At least they didn't drink and drive."

"They better not have puked on that fresh alfalfa I just bought," Addie said. "Who are those fellas?"

"Don't know their names," Hoyt said. "They're summer hands over at the Rocking J."

The cowboys were forgotten, as the three watchers noticed the occupants of the second abandoned truck sneaking from behind the barn toward their own vehicle. Mel figured the young couple couldn't be more than sixteen, and even from a distance she could see the girl's dress was on inside-out.

"*Madre de dios*," Addie said, reverting to Spanish, a primary language of her childhood, a bond she and her father continued to share. "*¿Quien eren?*"

"Oh Lordie," Hoyt said. "Their names might as well be Montague and Capulet. That's Mike and Sarah Howlett's girl and Tomás and Anna Trujillo's son."

"Been away, Hoyt. What's up with the Howletts and the Trujillos?" Mel asked.

"Ten years ago, during a blizzard, nearly a hundred head of Mike's steers broke through a fence and ended up in a box canyon on the Trujillo place. They bunched up so close, over half suffocated, leaving a helluva mess. Mike blames Tomás for not repairing his part of the fence, and Tomás blames Mike for leaving his dead cattle to rot in one of his best pastures. Came to blows once or twice, and sheriff's been worried for ten years about it turning into gun play."

Addie laughed. "Looks to me like the next generation just turned it into play."

They watched as the second pickup drove at a normal pace toward the ranch entrance. The two occupants waved shyly, with the trio returning the wave.

Hoyt let out a low whistle. "If Mike and Tomás end up with a grandbaby out of all this, let's pray they don't figure out where the deed was done."

Mel cocked her head to one side. "I don't know. Let's pray if there is a baby it will be a bridge to peace."

"Wishful thinking," Hoyt said.

Joe Bob walked directly to his boss, his face still red with anger. "I'm so sorry, Miss Addie. I never thought to check the barns for stragglers last night."

"That's okay, Joe Bob. Just one of the risks of a big party." Addie's face contorted into a disgusted grimace. "Don't tell me they puked in the new hay."

"Even worse...my favorite feed bucket. I'll be sterilizing that before I put out any feed this morning."

They all turned to Mel as she erupted into a full belly laugh.

"What's so funny?" Addie asked.

"If yesterday's party wasn't a legend already, it will be now." Mel used her sleeve to wipe away laughter induced tears.

Hoyt's chuckle set it off, and soon both he and Addie were laughing so hard that Addie dropped to her knees, her legs weak from laughter. Joe Bob looked at them all, obviously less than amused.

"Respectfully, you all can go to thunder. You don't gotta clean that bucket."

❦❦❦❦

Mel felt a new freedom as she rode side-by-side with Addie, both mounted on young horses in the process of training. Old Blue was back on pasture, and Mel was mounted on the same bay filly she was tasked to turn into a prize-winning reining and western pleasure horse. The young horse showed promise, and Mel secretly wondered if Addie would allow Mel to be the rider when the filly made her rounds of the horse shows. The young horse rode quietly, head slightly down, a drastic contrast to the paint horse colt Addie rode. He danced and pranced the entire first mile of the ride to the spring.

The difference between training for the shows compared to the rodeo circuit, Mel thought. The colt showed promise as well on barrels and pole bending. He was fast and agile, much like the paint mare who had carried Addie to her three-time wins as World Champion Cowgirl. He had the right urge to race just as the bay filly had the disposition for the precision and control so critical to performance events.

"Feels like we've gone back in time," Mel said.

"How's that?" Addie asked.

"Look at what we're riding. You on a fast paint and me on a steady bay, just like when we were in high school."

"Dang if you're not right."

Mel pulled the filly to a stop, letting Addie take the lead down the short piece of single file path down to the cottonwoods and water at the spring in the shallow valley below. As a natural racer, Mel knew the colt wouldn't handle well being forced into second place.

They rode to "their" cottonwood tree, where they dismounted and tied both horses to a low branch. Mel retrieved a thin blanket from where it was rolled and tied behind the cantle of her saddle. As soon as she'd laid and smoothed the blanket on the ground, she stretched full-length in the shade of the tree. She watched Addie as the dark-haired woman stood near the blanket, facing the ridge which harbored the path they had just used to descend from the almost desert prairie above, to the green solitude of the spring and its contained ecosystem. Addie continued to stare intently.

"What are you looking at?" Mel asked.

Addie pointed to the ridge. "We should build it there."

"Build what, where?"

Addie turned and looked at Mel. Her face expressed intense emotion, something Mel didn't expect on this leisurely ride to their sacred spring.

Addie took a deep, steading breath. "Our house."

Mel sat up, abruptly tensing. "What?"

"I said 'our house.' You deaf?"

"No, just surprised."

Addie dropped to a cross-legged seat on the blanket, facing Mel, her eyes studying her lover with an intensity that made Mel's breath catch in her chest.

"I mean it, Mel. Can you think of any place in the world you'd rather live?"

Mel bent her good leg to steady herself as she sat totally upright, facing Addie squarely. As she moved, her gaze left Addie's eyes and focused on the metal foot extending from the jeans covering her left leg. For a moment, she couldn't breathe, and she felt a totally unexpected panic. She jumped to her feet, only slightly unsteady on the artificial one. Walking rapidly toward the edge of the water, she dropped to her knees and scooped handfuls of the cold, clear water to coat her face and neck, ignoring the dampness of her shirt created in the process. She craved the cold, the sensation that told her she was alive, and this moment was real. As she knelt, Mel began to shiver as she struggled to give words to the wave of emotions. She didn't hear Addie as she approached. Mel didn't notice Addie's presence until she felt the comforting softness of the blanket placed across her shoulders and back.

"What was that about?" Addie asked, a hint of hurt in her voice.

Mel pulled the blanket close. "Addie, love, I'm broken."

"Hell, aren't we all broken in some way?"

The shivering began to subside. "Not, like this. It's not just my foot...not just knowing that the quality of the rest of my life depends on some contraption that serves as a poor substitute for my once whole leg."

"Then what is it? I love you, you big goof. None of that matters to me."

Mel turned. She opened the blanket, wordlessly inviting Addie into the comfortable warmth it offered. Despite the summer day, intensity of emotion left them both with a chill. Addie moved into her lover's embrace. Mel kissed Addie's neck as she gathered her thoughts, seeking to understand the tsunami of emotion she'd felt when Addie spoke the words "our house."

"Addie, darling, not even you can understand that I lost more than a foot and ankle that day. Forever, a piece of my heart, soul, and mind will always be lost in the rubble of that café." She took a shaky breath. "My ability to just live a normal life is crippled." Swallowing hard against a knot of fear in her throat, she continued. "Do you really want that? How can I possibly ask you to walk this road with me?"

Pulling back enough to look into Mel's eyes, Addie responded. "You didn't ask. I volunteered." She sighed. "Honey, there isn't, and never has been, anyone who could take your place in my life. I'll walk that road, good times and bad. What's the phrase in wedding vows…'for better or worse'? Besides, I'm no walk in the park either, you know."

Mel chuckled. "There's no safe answer to that."

"I know. Don't gloat."

"So, what do you mean 'our house'?"

Addie stood, pulling Mel to her feet along with her. "I mean I want to spend the rest of my life with you."

Mel realized there was a deep stillness inside, replacing the former panic. "I suppose you know some architect to help us make plans."

"Yep, back in California."

"You think he'll help?"

"Already called him. He'll be here next week."

Mel laughed so hard she scared into flight some crows perched in a nearby tree. "Yep, no walk in the park." She kissed Addie gently but briefly then turned away, a troubled expression replacing the flash of joy from just a moment earlier.

"What's wrong?" Addie asked.

"The boy, Hito."

"What about the boy?"

"Will there be a place for him in this house of ours?"

Addie punched Mel lightly on the arm. "Of course there's a place for him."

"If we find him."

A sigh was Addie's initial response, followed

by a silence as she searched for the right words. "My Linda, we have three investigators in Iraq looking for the boy. You're calling Sherine and that Lieutenant Canton so often Skype has them on the internet equivalent of speed dial. We're doing all we can."

"Is it enough? Enough to keep a promise to a dying mother?"

Addie stepped behind Mel, wrapping her arms around her. "Darling, maybe it's time for faith. I feel it in my bones that he's meant to be with us. Let it go for a while. Let the magic happen."

Mel turned, holding Addie close and burying her face in her lover's black hair. "Someone once told me that a fear is a wish—what we focus on is what we get. Maybe I need to let go of the fear and believe in the magic."

They stood in silence, just holding each other. Despite the almost absence of a breeze, there was a rustle of leaves and a lapping of water. If they'd known to listen, they might have heard the voices telling Mel that she was right.

❧ ❧ ❧ ❧ ❧

Addie felt the paint horse move beneath her, feeling the same familiarity she'd known with that mare as she carried her to so many wins and championships. They rode in the fine sunshine, going to the place Addie most loved in the world. As she topped the slight rise between the house and the small canyon where the spring nestled, she saw her father's pickup parked near the cliff edge overlooking the canyon. Not a quarter mile in the distance, she saw her mother, half-kneeling near the edge, a lever-action rifle already in place with the butt tucked against her shoulder, one elbow on her knee to steady the rifle barrel and improve her aim. Addie envisioned an imaginary line from rifle barrel to where a rider was preparing to descend into the canyon on the opposite side. It was Mel, the young Mel, the teenaged Mel, her Linda.

Responding immediately to the physical signals of a rider with whom she shared a psychic bond, the paint went from walk to full run in a heartbeat. Addie used the whip she rarely used on her beloved paint, begging for more speed, but they went nowhere. She felt the strain of the horse beneath her, giving her full heart to the speed she asked, but they went nowhere. The legs moved, both horse and rider leaned their bodies forward, seeking to cover ground, but they went nowhere.

The rifle gave a loud retort, and she saw Mel fall backwards off her bay's rump, pushed by the impact of a bullet.

Addie screamed, and sat upright in bed, the covers intertwined around her, nearly strangling her as her own weight prevented the sheet on her throat from allowing her to rise fully. The tension of the sheet eased as the woman beside her also rose, freeing more of the covers.

"What's wrong?" Mel yelled.

Addie couldn't answer. She placed her hands over her face, fighting to control the sobs that now racked her shaking body. Mel wrapped both arms around her lover. She gently placed a hand on the back of Addie's head, directing Addie to place her tear-streaked face on Mel's shoulder.

"Shh, darling. It was a dream. Just a dream," Mel

whispered.

"She did it. She shot you," Addie mumbled against her lover's shoulder.

"Ah, I see," Mel said. "Your dream freed the fear, gave it breath."

Addie leaned back, looking into Mel's eyes with an expression of surprise. "Is this what it's like...the dreams, the night terrors?"

"Yeah, pretty much," Mel said. "It's awful, but not really a bad thing. I guess for me, maybe for most people, it doesn't come until you feel safe."

"Why now?" Addie asked. She paused, and shook her head, striving to remember. "I had similar dreams a few times, in my twenties, but then"—she took a deep, shaky breath—"she never pulled the trigger."

As Addie started to shiver with emotion, Mel gently pushed her down to lie on the bed, and she pulled the covers up for both of them. She wrapped her whole body around her lover as Addie dealt with the cold of fear.

"Like I said, you're safe now. You can dare to face that old fear, to process it."

"I'm so sorry. I can't seem to quit shaking."

"It's okay, love. Will, my counselor, gave me an article that said shivering is a way of breaking up the chemicals and hormones triggered by the fight or flight reaction. It said that the body can sometimes store those chemicals for decades and shivering helps free them so they can be sloughed off by the body."

"So, when my woo-woo friends in California talk about body memory, they may be right?"

"Yeah, I guess so."

Addie was feeling warmer. Surprised, she noticed

that as the shivering gradually stopped, she felt free, like something had been emotionally healed.

Geeze, is this what Mel dealt with alone? Addie thought. She pulled Mel even closer as they both fell into a peaceful sleep.

Chapter Twenty-one

Unexpected Guests

A ddie opened the gate and four horses trotted sedately into the open horse pasture. *They must be as tired as I am*, Addie thought. Normally, the little herd would bolt full speed to their shared freedom, but horses and humans had worked hard the entire week. Mel was in the pasture, taking flakes of alfalfa from the bed of the Morris Ranch work pickup—the one that had been her father's last vehicle—and scattering hay for the horses, giving them the extra calories to help compensate for the hard work. Old Blue, the only horse exempt from the week's work duty, loped merrily up from the back of the pasture to share in the alfalfa treat, showing more energy that day than the much younger horses.

All cow/calf pastures on both ranches had been gathered and worked, including weaning, branding, and castrating calves as well as moving mamas to pastures distant from the weanlings' new homes where the young cattle would learn the joys and challenges of independent life. Every rancher knows the hard work of weaning time, equaling in effort the work and time needed nurturing a herd of heifers through their first calving. Mel, Addie, Hoyt, Sammy, Susan as camp cook, young Mellie, Addie's hired hands, and even the aging Alfredo had worked a week of long days, getting cows and calves gathered, sorted, and worked. Loss of sleep added to the exhaustion during the days when calves and mamas started in separate pens of headquarters' corrals, where they could be watched and cared for if the stress of weaning triggered any sign of illness. It was a noisy time with a constant cacophony of mamas calling for babies and vice versa. The experience was a part of cattle ranching Addie had not missed during her years in California.

Once the corral gate was closed, Addie walked around the pens and opened the wire gate that was the exit from the horse pasture. She laid the gate on the ground and watched as Mel drove slowly over the wire and into the yard of the Morris headquarters. Addie closed the gate and walked to the passenger door of the waiting pickup. It was only fifty yards or so to the house, but Addie preferred to ride at that moment. As she stepped into the truck, Mel looked at her, a tad slack-jawed with fatigue.

"If I were any more tired, I'd have tread and a valve stem," Mel said.

Addie reached to touch a strand of Mel's sweat encrusted hair where it showed below her hat. "You need to wash it soon. Your hair is starting to look like tire tread."

"You might want to wait until after a shower to look in the mirror yourself," Mel responded.

Mel punched the clutch smoothly, despite the artificial foot, and wrestled the gear stick into low. They crossed the yard, heading for the workshop where Mel would pull the truck inside and leave it to rest until the next dirty job needing a beat-up truck with four by four and a granny gear that was lower than low. She wasn't quite to the workshop when a gray sedan left the county road and turned into the driveway.

"Who's that?" Addie asked.

"Dang if I know."

Mel changed direction and pulled beside the sedan where it had parked in the drive beside the house. She cranked down the driver's window as the driver of the sedan did the same, albeit much more smoothly thanks to electric operation. The dark-haired woman inside did not look happy.

"Holy crap!" Mel said.

"Who is it?"

Mel turned her head abruptly, facing Addie. "Zadab."

"Your ex!"

"None other."

Mel and Addie exited the truck and walked toward the sedan. Zadab stepped out of the sedan as did another woman from the passenger side. Zadab leaned against the car, her arms crossed tightly against her chest. The other woman walked around the front of the car and moved to stand protectively beside Zadab. Her expression could best be described as a glare.

"I have a feeling I'm in big trouble for something," Mel whispered to Addie.

"Not with me," Addie said, a note of protectiveness in her voice.

"You haven't answered your phone in a week," Zadab said. She moved her arms so that she now rested a fist on each hip.

"Tower's been down so there hasn't been a signal. We've been weaning calves, so I haven't even bothered to turn it on." Mel paused, confused. "I haven't seen the message light blinking on the house phone."

"What house phone?" Zadab demanded.

Mel exhaled a long breath. "I guess it's the one I forgot to give you the number for."

"Yes," said the other woman. "Zadab has been worried sick."

Addie looked at the unidentified women. *Must be Zadab's lover. Bet watching her partner worry about an ex really hurt. It would me.*

"I truly am sorry, Zadab," Mel said. "This is one of the busiest times of the year, and I didn't even think I hadn't given you the number for the house phone."

"And email?" Zadab half spit out the words.

"Oh boy, haven't checked that either. Addie's been checking hers at least once a day 'cause of the private investigator who's in Iraq."

"Waste of your money," the unidentified woman said.

"Yes!" Zadab added.

Addie could feel the hair on the back of her neck bristle, for all the world like an angry dog. "It's my money, and it seems a good investment to me. We'll find that boy. You just wait."

Zadab laughed, a gesture that eased the tension in the air. "We have," she said.

"Have what?" Mel asked.

"Found the boy, you silly woman," said the unidentified woman.

Mel swayed, unsteadily. Addie stepped to her side and put an arm around Mel's waist. Zadab took a half step toward them, obviously thought better of it, and then leaned back against the car.

"My cousin, Sherine. She found him," Zadab said. "He is in an orphanage not far from Baghdad."

The color drained from Mel's face. She stood open-mouthed, tears filling her eyes and then spilling onto her cheeks.

"Is she sure?" Mel asked in a breathless voice.

"Yes, Melinda, she is sure." As the anger eased from Zadab's face, her voice gentled. She looked at Addie. "Your money was not totally wasted. Your investigator asked questions, tracking down the medics who responded that day. They did not trust him, but they did trust Sherine. Word had spread of a Navy officer, a woman, looking for the boy she'd rescued and that Sherine was helping with the search. He was silent with the detective, but he went to Sherine. From there, it was easy to track where the boy had gone."

Mel released a yell, a call, a primal vocalization so deep and intense it made the horses look up from their hay. Old Blue left the grazing and trotted to the fence, neighing loudly in concern. Addie held Mel tightly, and Mel turned into the embrace. Addie realized that tears covered her own cheeks, and it seemed perfectly natural when the other two women joined in a group hug, tears falling from their eyes.

Far away, a young boy awoke in the midst of a Middle Eastern night. He felt this inexplicable wave of love.

꧁꧁꧂꧂

The smell of strong coffee had yet to fight its way through the chemically induced sleep Mel had finally resorted to the night before. The bottle of prescribed pills remained untouched through the worst of her nightmares and terrors, but she felt no regret from seeking aid for sleep created by the excitement of hope. Addie's encouragement had helped.

Addie sat alone at the table, coffee cup and an empty oatmeal bowl before her. She used Mel's tablet to search airline and lodging possibilities to a place she'd never imagined she'd visit—Baghdad. The four of them sat around the table the night before, feasting on hastily made spaghetti and salad, discussing next steps. Addie helped Zadab and Leila bring their bags into the guest room while Mel cooked a quick meal, dancing with excitement before the stove, her artificial foot creating an odd percussion for the music she heard in her head. After dinner, they stayed at the table, going through the contents of a huge manilla folder Zadab and Leila had brought. It contained much of the critical information needed, including all the hoops to jump through—of which there were many— to travel to Iraq to visit the boy. Mel was determined to adopt, and all three of her companions were equally determined to help her through that process.

Zadab was the first to answer the olfactory caffeine call. She stumbled out of the guest room, hair awry, wearing satin pajamas. Addie glanced her direction as Zadab headed down the hall to the bathroom. Addie looked down at her own t-shirt and sweatpants and felt an instant of jealousy, wondering if Mel would prefer the silky feel of satin. The jealousy evolved into a smile as she switched her shopping from travel to lingerie, finding and ordering new pajamas. The smile came from the fantasy of surprising Mel, making the pajamas a potential gift for them both.

"The coffee smells good," Zadab said as she returned to the kitchen, still pajama clad. "Do you like it strong, like Melinda?"

"Of course, we both grew up with what our mothers called 'cowboy coffee.' Mel's dad used to say he used it to clean carburetors." Addie pointed to the cabinet above the coffee maker. "Cups are there, help yourself." She started to push back her chair. "What do you want for breakfast?"

Zadab waved her hands in gentle protest. "Not yet, please. Coffee first."

"Sure thing." Addie cocked her head to one side in concentration. "When you're ready, we have all you need for a Mediterranean breakfast like Mel makes. I like it."

Cup of black coffee in hand, Zadab took a seat at the table. "Good brown bread, olives, tomato, plain yogurt, and olive oil with spices for the bread?"

"You got it, except we can't find the right spices, so Mel uses Italian spices."

"I guess that would do."

Addie turned off the tablet, giving Zadab her full attention. "Mel still thinks the world of you."

"And I her. Are you okay with that?"

"Mostly," Addie said. "Getting easier now that I've met you. How about Leila?"

Zadab chuckled. "She is not yet to 'mostly.' It has helped that Mel wants to find this boy so badly. For her, Mel is becoming a person, but she still sees her as a rival for my heart."

"Is she?"

Zadab paused to take a long drink of coffee, studying Addie over the rim. Addie felt another twinge of jealousy as she saw the depth and beauty of Zadab's deep brown eyes.

"No more than I am for Melinda's heart. Don't you know she has always loved you? Many times, she told me of her first love. How do they say it...the one who got away?" She swirled the coffee in her cup, apparently thinking how to answer. "Mel will always be important to me. I think we were sure of each other more than we were ever in love. In our way, we both led dangerous lives. We needed something solid, dependable. Mel gave that to me, and I to her."

"Until you met Leila?"

A flicker of shame flashed across Zadab's face. "Even after that, but once I met her, I could no longer be happy with only the trust and strength I'd had with Melinda." She looked at Addie curiously. "I did not understand it at the time, but I think part of the reason Melinda and I worked was because both our hearts belonged to someone in the past."

"Who was yours?" Addie regretted asking as she saw a flicker of pain in Zadab's eyes.

"I was almost a child and barely a woman when my father was imprisoned and killed, some political complication I never fully understood. He secretly worked with the Americans, and one night, two men came to our door, telling my mother that we were in danger, and they were there to take us to safety."

"Who were they?"

"We never knew. They were American, but they spoke perfect Arabic. We barely had time to pack a single bag for each of us. We never saw our home again."

"You left someone behind?"

"Yes. We loved each other even as children. I tried to leave that night, to go to her, at least to say goodbye. I was not allowed. We did not know at the time, but my father was already dead, and the traffickers had targeted my mother and I."

"Human traffickers?"

"Yes. Had we not left that night, I would have most likely been sold to a Saudi."

"Did you give up hope of seeing her again?"

Zadab's face went still. She rose from the table and moved to the coffee pot, taking her time refilling her cup, her back to Addie.

"I managed to write to her and her to me, but the letters stopped after only a few months. It was years before I learned she died in a suicide bombing, much like the one where Melinda was injured."

"Jesus," Addie whispered.

Zadab turned, walking back to the table, her face studiously strong. "You can call on him for me if you wish, but I prefer Allah."

As Zadab returned to her seat at the table, Leila stumbled into the kitchen. Neither woman had heard her leave the guest room. Her hair was tousled, and she wore a bright red shorty version of Zadab's satin pajamas. The new arrival stepped behind Zadab, placing a kiss on top of her lover's head, and spoke in a throaty Arabic to Zadab.

"Anything I should know?" Addie asked, smiling. "If it's 'come back to bed,' I promise not to listen."

Both women laughed. "She said she's starving," Zadab explained.

Addie rose from the table, taking her bowl to the sink. "Mediterranean breakfast coming right up."

Mel hopped one legged into the kitchen in time to hear all three women laugh. She mirrored Addie's t-shirt and sweatpants. She grabbed the nearest kitchen chair and sat. Addie put a hand on each hip and scowled playfully at Mel.

"Couldn't you have at least put your foot on for company?"

"But then I'd have to help fix breakfast," Mel answered.

Addie looked directly at Zadab. "So, you just turned her over to me."

"Of course, otherwise I'd have to fix her breakfast."

Leila walked around the table toward Addie. "I'll help fix the breakfast before you women make me starve."

Chapter Twenty-two

A Dangerous Place

For the first time in her life, Addie totally understood the term "culture shock." Sure, she'd traveled. She'd spent four years the lover of a movie star and travel was part of the lifestyle, but never anything like this. Cancun didn't have concrete barriers, twelve feet tall, erected between the street and homes or commercial buildings—Mel had explained the need for protection from car bombs. Paris wasn't sprinkled with checkpoints where uniformed soldiers—some Iraqi and some American—scrutinized their papers like the soldiers' lives depended on it.

"Their lives and the lives of others do depend on it," Mel responded when Addie commented on their scrutiny.

It had taken weeks to get their visas, despite intercession by senior level military personnel on Mel's behalf. In the end, once again, it had been Sherine who provided the answer. A few phone calls from her, and an impassioned letter to the Iraqi embassy in Washington had provided the key to the four of them obtaining the most gorgeous visas Addie had ever seen in any passport. The design was incredible and as complex as the process required to obtain them. In the interim, Sherine had also been their emissary to the orphanage and to Iraqi agencies responsible for care of orphaned children. She'd even met the boy, Abdul. That was the only name he had. Even as a toddler, he knew his own name, but a last name eluded him. Any identification his parents had on them was lost in the confusion and destruction of the explosion that orphaned him.

Today was the day, the culmination of all their work, their plans, the anguish all four women had endured during the process. While Mel felt the brunt of it, this mission to find and protect one little boy had created a bond between Mel, Addie, Zadab, and Leila unlike any Addie had ever known before. Maternal instincts, perhaps the strongest of all human motivations, became a shared burden for the four women. Even Leila warmed to Addie and, eventually, even to Mel. The bond which held them together was a little boy, one whose picture, snapped by a visiting Sherine, now held a place of honor in the wallets and desktops of all four women.

Anxious and eager, the four women hadn't even taken a full day to recuperate from the demanding journey from the States to Baghdad, before they hired a car for the relatively short journey to the orphanage. Mel had driven in Iraq before, but she missed her assigned Humvee with the eagle emblazoned on the front plate, designating her rank, and assuring easy passage through any U.S. or ally-controlled area. Addie had been a little nervous that Mel would be able to concentrate behind the wheel, considering her obsession with seeing the boy, but, as usual, her lover proved her ability to overcome obstacles and do what needed to be done. They arrived safely with Sherine riding up front with Mel and the other three women packed into the backseat. At one time, it would have been an awkward arrangement, but Addie was surprised at how safe and comfortable she felt with Zadab, Mel's ex, so close. Love of a boy whom they'd never seen surpassed all hurdles, making the socially impossible possible.

They pulled into a dirt area which apparently served as the parking lot for the orphanage. Sherine had prepared them as best she could for what they would find. In a country torn for over a decade by war and conflict, orphans lived at the bottom of the social priority list. Abdul was lucky, being placed in one of the better institutions, run by a man and senior staff who somehow managed to find almost enough food and clothing, and even a few educational tools for the children entrusted to their care, but there was never enough money. The buildings of the complex were shabby and in need of repair. As they pulled up, Addie noticed a handful of horses—Arabians of course—in a pasture adjacent to the property, something she took as a good sign.

All five women exited the vehicle. Sharine's feet barely touched the ground before she was leading the way down a dirt-packed path to the front entrance. The remaining women started to follow when a sound caused them to freeze in place. The voice of a child sang loud and clear, and Addie shook her head at the incongruous juxtaposition of a familiar tune in a foreign place with foreign words. She turned to face Mel, whose expression was frozen in rapture. Addie followed Mel's gaze and saw a young boy standing beside the fence with the horses on the other side. Two mares and their young foals stood fascinated, the foals actually extending their noses through the fence, reaching to touch the singing boy.

Mel stepped away from the other women, walking several steps toward the boy, and waiting.

"Isn't that the tune to the song your mother—?" Addie started to ask, but she was interrupted as Mel sang loudly in a clear alto.

"Dapples and grays, pintos and bays, all the pretty little horses."

The child's voice drifted to a stop, and he turned in the direction of the other half of his duet.

"Way down yonder, in the meadow, all the pretty little horses," Mel sang, her voice fading to silence.

The boy did not hesitate. He ran with all his heart and amazing speed for his size and age, directly toward Mel. Seeing what was about to happen, Addie positioned herself behind Mel, placing her shoulder against Mel's back, striving to steady the woman. From four feet away, the running boy launched himself at Mel, and she caught him, embracing him with all her strength of body and heart. Despite Addie's help, they were forced back a step by the impact. The boy sobbed and spoke words Addie could not understand, but she recognized it was the same phrase over and over again.

"What's he saying?" Addie turned to Zadab, desperate for an answer.

"He's saying, 'I knew my angel would come. I told them she would come.'"

A huddle of women who gathered close shed a thousand tears, a small boy the epicenter of their joy and grief.

སྐ་སྐ་ᅟᅠ

The man watched through the fly-specked window of his office, little more than an oversized closet really. At the end of the day, there was little energy and even less money to spare for cleaning windows. Every dinar they could raise went to the children. Even at that, his heart broke when he walked the halls at night—ensuring all his charges were safe—and he could hear a voice or maybe voices quietly expressing the unique cry of hunger. He saw the boy, the one the other children teased about his coming angel, as the child ran across the lot, launching himself into the arms of a woman who should be a stranger to him.

"His angel?" the man whispered, no one there to ask but himself. "Perhaps." A tear escaped one eye, quickly running downward to hide within his beard. "Yes, his angel. I do believe in angels." The man watched intently as the contingent of women gathered around the boy and the woman who held him. *I do not wish to stand in the way of angels.*

Chapter Twenty-three

Gold in the Broken

The tiny office was filled to capacity and almost beyond. The four women sat in a group of mismatched chairs that had been acquired from other rooms, enabling them to sit during this crucial interview. As always, if Mel were anywhere close to him, the boy was in her lap, leaning against her and studying her fingers as though they held the meaning of life. Perhaps for him, they did. She was his angel. The man was pleased to also see how comfortable the boy was laying his legs and feet across the lap of the dark-haired American, including how the woman rested her hand gently on the boy's ankle. He was no fool. The man knew the nature of the two women's relationship and secretly thought the boy lucky to have two such women ready to take him into their hearts and their home. He knew also that every day spent in Iraq put their lives at risk, a thought that kept him up most nights since their arrival.

Sitting at his old and battered desk, the man looked at the papers spread before him. It had been a little over a week since the four women came to his door, turning his little orphanage into a bevy of hushed whispers among children, staff, and volunteers who watched events progress with rapt attention. Never before had an American come to adopt a child there, much less a woman with no husband, a crippled US Veteran. Some wanted to hate her, but even the most dedicated American hater could not help but be touched by the obvious love between the woman and the boy. The story spread of how she'd saved him, dragging him from the rubble, despite her own severed foot. Her presence was making a difference. Zadab and Leila's proficiency in Arabic helped as well. Soon all four visitors joined volunteers in cooking and cleaning, wiping runny noses, changing diapers. They'd arrive each day with a fresh load of different things from the Baghdad markets and shops. For once, there was enough food. One day, the four women asked permission to measure the children for shoes. By the next day, no child went barefoot on the rough floors of the orphanage nor on the hot earth outside.

"I hope the guardian process takes a very long time," a senior staff member told the man one evening as they watched the car the Captain (for that is what they now called Mel) drove leave, back to the hotel where the women stayed.

The man smiled, but he thought differently. He knew that being in Baghdad put the women in danger. He knew also that having Americans in his orphanage could put his children in danger as well. That had been the argument he'd used that finally got the attention of the bureaucrat overseeing whether or not Mel would be allowed to adopt the boy she'd saved.

"I have received the decision of the Bureau of Citizenship about your petition for guardianship for Abdul." He cleared his throat. "As you know, Iraqi policy does not allow a child to go to anyone of a faith that was not that of his family."

Zadab leaned forward, tapping on the papers on the man's desk. "Then I will petition. I am Muslim."

The man raised his hand, gently silencing Zadab before she launched into a complete speech.

"That will not be necessary." He spoke English clearly, despite a heavy accent. Opening a small, brown envelope on his desk, he pulled a necklace from inside and held it by the chain so all four women could see. It was a crucifix. "We tracked down the same medic who sent you to us and learned that this was found around his mother's neck."

All four sets of eyes sparkled with new hope. The man could have sworn the room became brighter. Even the boy felt the energy. He dropped Mel's hand and looked to the man.

"What does that mean?" Mel asked.

The man laughed gently, a pleasant sound in his deep, bass voice. "It means, Captain, that the boy is yours to guard, to love, to raise."

The already full room nearly exploded with the calls of joy from the women. The boy sat up, looking surprised and confused. Zadab leaned toward him, telling him in rapid Arabic that Mel would be his mother. The boy yelled in joy, threw his arms around Mel's neck, and squeezed so hard, the man was afraid she couldn't breathe.

"You may take him with you today, although the children and my people would be very upset if they don't have a chance to say goodbye."

"They'll have their chance." Mel glanced at the other women. "We've been hopefully planning a party."

"With your permission, good sir, we have gifts for the children and the staff," Zadab said.

Another laugh escaped from the man's deep bass voice. "Of course. That would be wonderful."

Excited, the women shuffled awkwardly from the tiny space and into the hallway. Despite her artificial foot, Mel managed to join the boy as they skipped down the hallway toward the room he shared with ten other boys. He didn't have much, but now they could take with them the things that were his. He belonged with Mel and Addie, even with Zadab and Leila.

The man watched them leave then glanced both ways down the hallway to ensure no one was close before he returned to the chair behind his desk. From a drawer, he withdrew a small, cheap jewelry box and a sales receipt showing he had paid in cash, stuffing them into his briefcase. When he got home that night, he would burn them.

❧❧❧❧

A steady drone from the wide-bodied jet had lulled most of the passengers to sleep. A few watched a movie on the screens that had dropped from the ceiling, listening through earphones purchased from the flight attendants. Zadab and Leila slept peacefully, sharing one blanket, Leila's head resting on Zadab's shoulder and Zadab's check comfortably placed against Leila's hair. Mel stared at the boy whose head rested in her lap. He drooled slightly as he slept, and she thought it a beautiful sight. The majority of his small body lay in his own seat, and his stocking feet were comfortably placed in Addie's lap. Mel looked at her lover and noticed with surprise that Addie was awake, looking at Mel with a soft smile and eyes expressing a melancholy happiness.

"Are you happy, Mel?"

"Happier than I would have thought possible just a few months ago. You?"

"Me?"

"Are you happy?"

"So much so, it's almost painful." Addie tucked a piece of blanket around Abdul's leg where a small patch of bare skin was exposed. "And a little scared. I never thought I'd be raising a child. Of all the things I've done, this is the scariest."

Mel's breath caught for a moment. "Having second thoughts?"

"Oh God no." She bit her lip gently, obviously striving to find the right words. "It's kinda like looking into the Grand Canyon. It's so big that I feel tiny."

Mel laughed quietly, striving not to disturb the sleeping passengers. "I know what you mean."

They were already holding hands, the combined pair resting on the boy's chest. At some point in his sleep, the boy had slipped a hand from the covers, adding a third to the stack. Addie rubbed a thumb gently across the top of Mel's hand. She looked pointedly toward Mel's left leg.

"Will this...will this help heal...well?"

Mel chuckled. "Heal my leg? The foot will always be gone. Nothing fully replaces that. Heal the nightmares? It will help, but there will always be a part of me stuck in the rubble of that café."

"I'm sorry I can't help fix that."

"Oh, but you do, my love. You do." Mel shook her head, looking without seeing at one of the movie screens. "You know what the Japanese do when a precious dish is cracked, when it will be forever scarred?"

"What?"

"They fix it with gold, filling the crack with something more precious than the dish itself." Gently, Mel extracted both their hands from the boy's and raised Addie's to her lips, kissing it softly. "I've found my gold."

Exhaustion overcame them both soon thereafter. Their intertwined hands returned to the boy's chest. Without waking, he once again placed his tiny hand on top of his parents'.

Epilogue

In Due Time

A ddie herself led the chestnut stallion into the two-horse slant trailer, securing the lead of his halter to a metal ring bolted into the wall of the trailer.

"It will be a long trip, young fellow, but I do believe you will make your papa proud," she said as she rubbed the jaw of the young horse.

As Addie stepped away from the horse, Mel swung the hinged panel closed, effectively enclosing the horse into one stall of the trailer. Both women exited out the open back, and the groom closed the double back doors of the trailer and secured the latch. Everything was loaded, ready for the three-day trip to Kentucky, stops already identified along the way so the young horse could be boarded overnight in comfort. Despite conception from the frozen sperm of his long-dead sire, Run 'Em Down was perhaps the most promising of the hundreds of foals Flag 'Em Down had fathered. The young horse seemed to understand something major was underway, but he remained calm, in contrast to the disposition of many Thoroughbreds. Addie attributed the legendary disposition of Romero Ranch's horses to the gentle techniques Mel brought to the early handling and halter training of all their young horses. She was so pleased that their son showed the same magical skill. Addie and Mel made no secret of their pride in the magnificent young man Abdul had become. In his third year of veterinary school, both women were eager for his graduation and return to the ranch. At different times, they'd both made it clear he was free to pursue whatever dream fed his soul, but he'd never wavered from a vision of adding his own magic to the legendary Romero Horse Ranch. Sammy had already lifted much of the burden from Hoyt's shoulders in the operation of the Morris Ranch. In the decades since Addie and Mel made their relationship legal during a quiet ceremony beside the waters of their precious spring, the lines between the two ranches had blurred and blended so that all involved felt like one family. Sammy obviously retained the Morris talent for horses, cattle, and business, and Abdul obviously retained the horse talents of both his mothers.

"Are you sure he's not biologically yours?" Addie would sometimes tease her wife.

"Not biologically, but I am his angel."

"As you both keep reminding me," Addie said with feigned envy.

Once the stallion was loaded, both women stood back, looking at the trailer, contemplating the possibility of Addie accomplishing another record by becoming a two-time owner of a Kentucky Derby champion. *Maybe this time I'll get that Triple Crown,* she thought, not expressing that secret dream even to Mel.

Mel was wearing her "dress" foot, which also enabled her to don both of the boots comprising the expensive pair of hand-made beauties Addie had given Mel for Christmas. Mel leaned slightly on the cane she carried. The cane was not so much because of the prosthesis as it was from the explosion's injury that had not reared its ugly head for many years. Dizziness sometimes surprised her, the result of the damage to her inner ears.

"Does it feel like when you took his daddy to the Derby?"

"A little," Addie answered. "But my hair didn't have gray in it back then."

Mel reached up to caress a strand of her wife's hair. "Beautiful then and beautiful now."

"Compliments, compliments! After all these years, I'd think you'd have figured out you don't have to kiss my butt to get laid."

"Oh honey, I did figure that out. I just enjoy telling my wife she's beautiful."

Someone cleared his throat behind them. Both women turned to face the groom who would be driving the truck with the trailer, the jockey riding shotgun. His face flushed beet red, leaving no doubt that he'd heard the conversation.

"Are we ready to go, Miss Romero?" he asked.

"Yeah, Robbie, you go ahead. Mel and I will follow in the SUV."

"Yes, ma'am." The jockey was already in the truck. The groom did a full 360 walk around the vehicle and trailer, checking tires and hitch as he did so. His attention to detail was what caused Addie to select him for the trip.

"That's a good boy," Mel said.

Addie looked at Mel, her eyes squinted. "Boy? He's forty-five if a day."

"I find that designation of who is young has changed for me over the years."

"I hear that," Addie said.

They walked toward the SUV, and Addie did the same routine around that vehicle while Mel climbed into the passenger seat. They would be following the truck and trailer for the entire trip. Abdul and Lupe, his fiancé, would fly out just before the race to be with "the moms." As Addie took her place in the driver's seat, Mel leaned over and placed her hand over Addie's, halting her from triggering the ignition.

"How badly do you need this win?" Mel asked.

Addie turned to face her wife. "A win would be good. We still have some room in the trophy case, and stud fees would be something fine to pass on to Abdul."

"But you don't have your heart set on it? Odds are against a second win, you know."

"Oh, I'll be disappointed for a while if that happens." She grasped Mel's hand, carrying it to her lips and kissing the palm. "I found everything I really need a long time ago." She hadn't put on her seatbelt yet, so it was easy to slide across the seat and give her lifemate a long kiss. "You're not the only one who found your gold, you know."

If you liked this book?

Reviews help an author get discovered and if you have enjoyed this book, please do the author the honor of posting a review on Goodreads, Amazon, Barnes & Noble or anywhere you purchased the book. Or perhaps share a posting on your social media sites or spread the word to your friends.

Author's Note:

Like any novelist, I pray you readers enjoyed and valued the journey within the pages of this book. As it ends, I want to write to you, personally, on a serious note. Part of the inspiration to write *Broken* happened a few years ago when I found myself in an odd situation when I was the only one with any clue how to comfort a strapping young man, fresh out of the Marines and home from Afghanistan, when he sobbed uncontrollably, trying to express the pain and need caused by his memories. It was then that I realized I had to do my small part in comforting those who suffer from PTSD—and not just Veterans—with the assurance that they weren't alone, and to educate those who love them with hints of how to provide the love and support they long to give.

Early in this book Mel makes a promise to Hoyt, a promise not to give up, no matter what.

For those of you suffering from intense PTSD or any form of depression, make the promise. Maybe to a brother or sister, a spouse or lover, a comrade in arms, a friend, a parent, a counselor, a child…whoever, but make that promise. It can combat the desire to resort to a horrific and permanent solution to a temporary problem.

About the Author

As a writer and consultant, Kayt C. Peck has worked with many diverse organizations over the years. She found wisdom in the words and lives of people of all colors, religious beliefs, sexual orientations, gender identities, nationalities, and socio-economic classes. Her life-long career as a writer has included working as a journalist, a public-affairs officer in the U.S. Naval Reserve, and as a grant expert, writing applications raising more than $30 million for worthy domestic and even international organizations. She has published several novels, one biography, and written many plays, including being a two-time awardee in the Rocky Mountain Voices play competition and receiving a special award for Excellence in Play Writing at the American Association of Community Theatres Region VI 2015 finals. She has authored and published numerous articles, short stories, and poems. The first edition of *Kiva and the Mosque* and her novel, *Good Water*, were both finalists in the New Mexico/Arizona Book Awards. Today, she lives quietly in her cabin home in the mountains of northeastern New Mexico.

Other books by Kayt

Good Water- ISBN- 978-1-939062-87-1

The dry plains drew Judy Proctor like a bear to her den…or a moth to the flame. Ranching was her life. The sweat as she branded or "doctored" cattle…the howl of a coyote in the quiet, night air...half-frozen fingers as she cut the wire to loosen hay bales for hungry cattle scratching for survival in snow-covered land…all of the everyday existence on the ranch was her life. It was where she belonged. It was a lonely life.

She had tried to leave the ranch to join the "normal" existence of a talented young woman in the city, but it had never been home. When her parents were killed in an automobile accident, she returned to the family ranch as much because she needed it as it needed her. She faced a lonely life to be shared with no better company than Somegood and Useless, her cow dog and the mottled mutt that were her companions.

Kathleen Romero slipped into Judy's life unexpectedly. She came to the plains to write a story. Would she stay because of the real truth she found in the simple drama of husbanding land and animals?

Unfortunately, even wide-open spaces can be plagued by prejudice and closed-minds. As the two women struggle to know each other, they must also carve a place for themselves among the country-folk who have been Judy's friends and neighbors her entire life.

The Ladies Room - ISBN - 978-1-943353-09-3

A dream is housed in the dusty, unused storage room above the Pink Triangle, one of Amber, Texas' two gay bars. Journalist April Sims serves as the reluctant leader in making that dream a reality. Under her guidance an eclectic group of women build a safe place in a community where being a lesbian can be dangerous and difficult.

April meets Sophia Mendez, a local attorney, as she seeks legal guidance for members of the group. In meeting with the women of the Ladies' Room, Sophia finds herself dealing with personal as well as professional issues.

When a radical religious group levels an attack on the entire gay community, even to the the point of a vigilante attack on the Pink Triangle, the strength and unity of the women of The Ladies' Room will be tested to the core.

Only time will tell if the beauty of the dream can override the ugliness of a harsh reality.

Prairie Fire - ISBN – 978-1-943353-47-7

Judy and Kathleen were accepted, even loved, by their conservative ranching neighbors. Their world felt safe and secure…until…until prairie fire! The flames disrupted their lives, causing destruction and injury, but the community pulled together to face a common enemy. When Kathleen's unofficial "daughter" found herself homeless, Pookie joined that community, bringing to this simple world her black clothes and rebellious nature. Together, conservative and liberal, gay and straight, they were a community, ready to face fire itself. The surprise to them all was the unseen enemy from within, one that had the potential to destroy them all.

The Kiva and The Mosque - ISBN - 978-1-943353-85-9

In a troubled world, answers rarely come from where they are expected. The need for answers to save a troubled humanity forces Kidwell Brown and Aisha Sudda, two total strangers, into roles they never could have anticipated. Kidwell and her life-partner, Anna Montoya, live a quiet life in their mountain home until the day Kidwell is drawn to visit the ceremonial cave at Bandelier National Monument. Hundreds of miles away, Aisha Sudda Fletcher lives another quiet existence, along with her husband, Greg, until the day she is drawn to visit a garden beside a vandalized mosque.

On that day, both Kidwell and Aisha are chosen. These humble women soon learn that the time of prophets has not yet passed. During mystical moments, each woman is given a message – "Desert Lightning has no power" to Kidwell, and "The scimitar has no edge," to Aisha. They each pass along the message as instructed, neither realizing they have predicted important moments in world history.

Their mystical guides direct the women to "find their allies," and so the lives of Kidwell, Aisha, Anna and Greg are forever intertwined. They will face victory and exile, mystery and certainty.

In the end the very nature of humanity proves to be the world in which they must fight and survive.

As an unabashed advocate for the gay/lesbian/bisexual/ transgendered community in places were being different was dangerous, Kayt honed her skill in standing her ground and doing the right thing. Her entertaining and thought-provoking novels offer readers a rich banquet of characters, settings and scenarios that leave us both satisfied and wanting more.

Best-selling author Anne Hillerman

The Pyramid and the Painting - ISBN - 978-1-948232-13-5

Great magic comes with great gifts and great burdens. Kidwell and Anna must face together the ramifications of being thrust into world-changing roles. such responsibility exacts a price in their own lives and the many lifetimes they've shared before. The magic Kidwell and her co-prophet, Aisha, stumbled into in the first book in the series, Kiva and the Mosque, continues to push them all into situations they never could have imagined. As their life-partners, Kidwell's Anna and Aisha's Greg, must find their own strength and fight their own battles.

Not even great magic can prevent or cure a broken heart, but, sometimes, a broken heart is the only key to even deeper magic. Through great pain, Kidwell faces a transformation that has a profound effect not only on their lives but many lives across many worlds.

The Past & The Present - ISBN - 978-1-948232-87-6

The culmination of a tale spanning lifetimes thrusts the current lives of Kidwell, Anna, Maolan, Martin, Aisha, and Greg into an adventure that crosses not only millennia but also magical boundaries between worlds. A handful of humans joins with others—most viewed as only magical fantasy in the human world—to lead the fight to overcome great evil and to end a battle begun before any remembered human history. This group of mismatched and diverse heroes faces the unimaginable as a family. It is the love, caring, forgiveness, and courage they share that provide hope not just for themselves but for the world around them. The magic Kidwell and her co-prophet, Aisha, stumbled into in the first books in this series, The Kiva and the Mosque and The Pyramid and the Painting, continues to dominate all their lives. They face together not only great evil but their own doubts and weaknesses. With luck and determination, they may save not only the world but themselves as well.

Other books by Sapphire Authors

Last First Kiss: A Passport to Love Romance – ISBN – 978-1-948232-95-1

Alessia Cavalii is a rising star in the competitive international wine scene, and one of only twenty-six female master sommeliers in the world. Her home is a renovated winery on the windswept coast of Italy, she has a career she loves, and she is finally free of a toxic relationship. But Alessia is hiding a dangerous secret— one that could, in a second, shatter the life she's built. Parker Haven is a captain in the U.S. Army and stationed at the NATO military camp near Salerno. An investigator with the Military Police, she's pulled in to help solve a string of murders in the city and finds herself inexplicably drawn into Alessia's world. As the intrigue surrounding the case—and the alluring Alessia—spins more and more out of control, Parker realizes she may have to choose between her military career and the woman she's falling for. Do we ever truly know the people we love?

A storm's brewing on the horizon. Can Addie and Greyson weather it, or will it blow them over?

Blueprint for Romance: A Garriety Romance – ISBN – 978-1-948232-71-5

After the death of her husband, Dylan Lake's ability to trust in others is shattered. Her life is thrust into turmoil between caring for Emma, her seven-year old handicapped child, and working hard to make ends meet. Dylan doesn't have time to pursue a romantic relationship. Finding that one special person only happens in dreams. When fate keeps throwing Dylan and Kat together, Dylan finds her attraction to Kat something she can't ignore. Will her trust issues stop her from letting Kat into her and Emma's life? Leaving her old job and moving halfway across the country were the scariest things Kat Anderson had ever done. Starting a new life and career takes priority over any foolish notion of a fairy-tale future of romance and love. Kat's attraction to Dylan is time taken away from building a new business. Can Kat juggle love and duty to find her Happy Ever After? Welcome back to Garriety, the town with an open heart, and home to some of the quirky and warm characters from Add Romance and Mix. Join Kat and Dylan on their quest for true romance with a little help from Kat's sister Briley and her family, along with a host of new characters.

To Be Loved – ISBN – 978-1-948232-79-1

A dead body, women and kids in peril, treachery at every turn—no problem for the close-knit sexagenarian friends of the Silver Series, Dory, Robby, Jill and Charlene! When a calm evening walk leads Dory to suspect bad news is happening right next door in her placid neighborhood, and when a waif comes under Jill's wing, routine life takes a vacation. And when a corpse points toward a suspect who's far from virginal in character, and seems to link to the waif and the bad news, well! All bets are off. The women rally to defeat evil and correct injustice, helped with a generous serving of karma from a very unexpected source. Along the way, they work with and for the police, sometimes in—ah, unorthodox—ways. But what are a few more gray hairs to law enforcement when the cause of justice is advanced? They encounter smugglers in the devil's oldest crime, street-smart kids wiser than their years, maids in distress, and unlikely allies in Skid Row. But the persistent four also marshal the vengeance of the angels, through their own.

Bobbi and Soul – ISBN – 978-1-948232-41-8

Bobbi Webster wants nothing more than to be the best family practice doctor for her home town in rural Oregon. To accomplish that, she's enrolled in a two-year fellowship in rural medicine at Valley View Medical Center in Colorado. Sparks fly when Bobbi meets the Reverend Erin O'Rouke, a petite, feisty priest who meddles in the treatment of Bobbi's patients. To make matters worse, Bobbi wants nothing to do with any religion, much less the woman she dubs, The Elf.

Erin serves as vicar at a small church where a few parishioners have stipulated that she must be celibate, reflecting their "love the sinner, hate the sin" tactic. After she clashes with Erin, Bobbi recognizes how a recent breakup of an abusive relationship has falsely colored her perception of Erin's world and work. Likewise, when Erin understands how Bobbi's emotional wounds make her vulnerable, her natural empathy moves her closer to Bobbi.

They find themselves drawn to each other, but how can Bobbi and Erin overcome so many obstacles to find love?

Made in the USA
Columbia, SC
30 September 2020

21829361R00145